I0730239

Also by Joseph K. DeRosa

Books

Vera's Story: Escape to Freedom

Short Stories

Chatham 02633-2013

Chatham 02633-2014

Contributor

Medium.com

PleaseSeeMe.com

Visit

jkderosa.com

Praise for House on Main Street

"DeRosa weaves an impressively coherent narrative of best plans gone wrong in this story of love, loss, and how quickly we become victims of our follies. A woeful tale—with a ghost to boot. Caused me a sleepless night."

—Peggy Hinaekian, Author of *The Girl from Cairo*

"In the midst of a suicidal midlife crisis, Cliff Stone visits his family's old haunt on Cape Cod and is launched into a violent, drug addled, sometimes romantic adventure. Read this book, there's suspense, mystery, humor, and real history too.

—Mickey J. Corrigan, author of *What I Did for Love*

"With snappy dialogue and evocative language, we follow a man at the end of his tether, a ghost, two desperate women, and a contraband deal gone bad—all in a dilapidated mansion on old Cape Cod. Fresh and darkly hilarious, The House on Main Street defies the predictable."

—Sharon Millar, Author of *The Whale House and Other Stories*

"The House on Main Street by Joseph K. DeRosa is a wonderfully written book—highly recommended. I was totally with Cliff Stone, when he entered the old house, reminiscing about the summers he'd spent there with his ex-wife and children. Believing the house would give him his needed sense of solace, he walked across the threshold into a totally unexpected world."

—Jacquie Herz, Author of *Circumference of Silence*

The House on Main Street

A Novel

By

Joseph K. DeRosa

ff

fortissimo books

Concord, Massachusetts

The main portion of this book is a work of fiction. Names, characters, places, and incidents are the product of the author's imagination and are used fictitiously. Any resemblance to actual events, locales, or persons, living or dead, is coincidental. The Addendum is the true story of the house that inspired the main story.

ISBN 978-1-7329849-2-9

ƒƒ

fortissimo books
An Imprint of
Chatham House LLC
Concord, Massachusetts

Dedicated to
Robin & Peter

Contents

The House on Main Street

The secret to life is meaningless unless you discover it yourself.

—W. Somerset Maugham, *Of Human Bondage*

Ah, distinctly I remember it was in the bleak December,
And each separate dying ember wrought its ghost upon the floor.

—Edgar Allen Poe, *The Raven*

CHATHAM HOUSE

If only I hadn't crossed the Sagamore Bridge. I left my Back Bay apartment that cold December Sunday with no idea where I was going. Drove south with all the consciousness of a crash dummy. Woke up when I got to the Cape Cod Canal.

The bridge over the canal makes a high arc above the water. I've read the sign at the approach a hundred times—*Feeling Desperate? Call the Samaritans.* I was beyond desperate. Jumping off the bridge would be sure death. Fortunately, a high chain-link fence capped with barbed wire prevented a jump. I wanted my suicide to scream out my pain to the world—I just didn't want to die in the process. I needed a combo suicide and rescue.

With little traffic on the narrow bridge, I slowed and glanced down at the waterway far below. I've always marveled at the magnificent view of the canal—a straight cut that severed the Cape Cod peninsula from the mainland.

That peninsula juts eastward into the Atlantic, then bends north like a muscleman's flexed arm. Frigid arctic waters run down the forearm, while the warm Gulf stream flows up into the triceps. They mix into turbulent waters at the elbow where I was headed—the tiny fishing village of Chatham.

For centuries, confused fish swimming in those waters have been harvested by eager fishermen, and in fates dictate, shipwrecked fishermen have met their own untimely ends upon Chatham's shifting bars.

I always felt an affinity for Chatham—not because of fishing. I don't like blood and guts. I like to think about the indigenous people who lived there, the explorers who came, the pilgrims who settled. They all fished these waters, but a history professor makes his living fishing in the past, communing with ghosts.

I've perused the headstones at the seaside cemetery. They carry the names of early English settlers and occasional French explorers who married locals. No stones mark the graves of the indigenous peoples, even though they lived there for hundreds of years before the Europeans came. In a blink of history's eye, they vanished from their lands. Maybe their bones were plowed under by eager farmers, and the only homage paid them is that today, tourists sip drinks at places with names like *Monomoy* and *Wequassett*.

Once I crossed the bridge, I knew I'd end up in Chatham. What I didn't know was my fate was sealed—like those natives, those explorers, those settlers, and even those fish. Life has a way of changing unpredictably on the Chatham shoals.

I drove down Main Street through the center of town. Many of the shops and galleries were closed for the season, but the Squire Tavern was open for business. One of the cars parked out front had a bumper sticker that said, "Chatham: a quaint drinking village with a fishing problem."

I knew well what lay ahead. In about a thousand yards, Main Street took a sharp right and ran south along the ocean. A few narrow, dead-end streets led down to the beach. A half-mile up the steep incline was the bluff from where the ever-present beacon of the lighthouse scans the horizon. I had stood in front of the Coast Guard station on that bluff many times.

Below the lighthouse bluff, huge boulders prevented erosion of the cliffs, and beyond the boulders, rolling sand dunes stretched out to the tip of Monomoy, forming the elbow of the Cape. It is around the waters off Monomoy that the north and south currents mix, and the shoals constantly shift.

If I made that sharp right on Main Street, the character and mood of that section of Chatham would be very different. The shops, candy stores, and art galleries of the town center would be left behind, and I would be immersed in the Old Village, where, in earlier days, most of the residents were seafaring.

In those days, it was called Scrabbletown. Unscrupulous characters lurked in little shanties among the sailors, tradesmen, and fishermen. On a stormy night before the lighthouse was built, these so-called Mooncussers might move the signal lanterns that sat at the top of the bluff, so they could loot any unfortunate ship that wrecked on the Chatham bars. More often, on a seemingly harmless night, a sailor could get drunk at the Squire and wake up the next morning on a ship bound for China or the West Indies.

Just as I drove past the Squire, my heart pounded as if a powerful force was screaming at me, "Hazards ahead! Go no further." I slowed to a stop, and a loud horn blared, forcing me to pull over. I sat there with the motor running, trying to decide what to do.

Once I turned that corner, not too far up on the right, I would come across the old house on Main Street—it was calling me like a siren calling an ancient mariner to his demise. My sadness was seeking despair. When I saw it again, I would be at the edge of the vast Atlantic—not a good place for someone fantasizing about suicide.

Dostoevsky's Raskolnikov lamented that he'd rather wait on a narrow precipice for a thousand years than meet his immediate doom. I was waiting in my car a thousand yards away from a turn that could make me meet mine. Not ready for that, I shut off my engine.

The windshield immediately began clouding up, blotting out the winter sky that hovered low and gray, unlike the ever-loftier blue skies of the summers Penny and I used to spend in Chatham—in that house. How different today was. How different my life was compared to when we first came to Chatham eight years ago.

That year, we had rented a cottage on the warm-water side in South Chatham. My daughter was three then, and my son was one. We made sand castles on the beach and played in the mud flats at low tide. That was one of the happiest summers of my life, and we capped it off in September by buying a new house.

We hadn't planned to do so. One Sunday, we went apple picking in the country. The leaves were just beginning to turn auburn and yellow, and we saw an open house sign in front of a dream home—out of our league—but then, we were just enjoying the day.

The new saltbox colonial was designed by a craftsman builder to look like it dated back to colonial times. I explained to Penny that those farmers were smart. They extended the second-story roof down over a first-floor extension on the north side of the house.

"Vegetables and meats were stored inside the cold back wall like a little saltbox," I said.

"I didn't know that," was Penny's reply.

"See how they spaced the clapboard siding all around the house? The boards are closer near the ground to resist rotting when they piled manure along the foundation to generate heat."

Penny was impressed that I knew so much about colonial times, and I liked to show off my knowledge.

"Paul Revere lived in a similar-looking house in Boston."

"Do you know everything?" she asked.

"I know he got bagged by the Brits not far from this dream house. You know the poem The Midnight Ride of Paul Revere?"

"Yeah."

"Well, either Longfellow didn't know or didn't care that Revere's buddy Sam Prescott finally delivered the British-are-coming alarm to Concord. Maybe it was poetic license. Sam Prescott isn't as mellifluous as Paul Revere. Wasn't the first time credit went to the wrong guy. Won't be the last."

In those days, Penny liked my humor as well as my knowledge.

She and I both wanted to get out of our little house at the bottom of the big hill in Winchester. The roof leaked and the cellar collected stormwater in big rains. The new baby had moved into my study, and I did not find the smelly diaper pail conducive to my continued scholarship. Could we afford this dream house?

I was starting my first teaching job at the university; Penny was working the late shift at the hospital. She watched our daughter and son by day, and I took over at night. We screwed our courage together and made an offer. Things were as bright and hopeful for me that day as they were the day Penny walked down the aisle and greeted me with her wide smile and a big "Hi."

The builder accepted our offer, and we sold our old house. Thank God it happened on a sunny day during a sunny week.

We moved the kids into our dream house.

That was probably the last good year we had.

A cold chill came over my whole body. I started the engine and turned the heat up to max. I left the window defogger off, preferring to stay in my own cocoon to think.

Penny and I had struggled financially for a couple of years—no movies, not even pizza take-out, never mind a summer vacation. Not until my daughter was five, did we decide to return to Chatham, but Penny and I were too late making summer plans to get on the warm-water side.

Chatham. A magnificent house across the street from the beach.

That was what the ad in the Boston Globe said. We called right away. The owner, a Mrs. Thompson, now lived with her daughter off-Cape. Three bedrooms, two bathrooms, a huge shed out back. We took it, sight unseen, not knowing what to expect.

The house had the look of a haunted mansion—a large square box, each side as long as a Greyhound bus, rising two stories above its red brick foundation—ivy creeping up its sides.

From the day I first walked in, I was enthralled by the historic grandeur of the place: the dining room with its high ceiling of contoured tin, rough-cut pine floorboards, a pass-through from the kitchen, glass doorknobs, and flowered wallpaper over horsehair plaster walls.

I even loved the Cape Cod cellar, dug out years after the house was built. One section had dirt walls like a World War I foxhole. The other had a cement floor to accommodate an old furnace and support columns under giant, hand-hewn floor beams.

The attic rivaled the cellar. To get up into the Mansard eaves, you pulled out what looked like a small set of knick-knack shelves built into the wall. They became a step ladder to an attic hatch. There, a Lincoln Log bonanza of more hand-hewn beams crisscrossed the attic.

I felt a visceral attachment to the bones of that house—as much as my flesh felt to my own bones.

My daughter called it Chatham House, and the name stuck. The beach across the road numbed little legs wading in its waters, but the location had its compensation—we could easily walk to the center for ice cream.

For five consecutive summers, we returned to Chatham House, and I got to know its quirks and its secrets. The old house was built in 1850. Since then, it had stared relentlessly across Main Street at the cold waters to the east and had stood watch over all who passed its way—families, lovers, and loners traveling to and from Lighthouse Beach by day—as well as all the ships that passed in the night.

Each year I asked old Mrs. Thompson if she would sell it to me.

She said she would, but not just yet.

During those years, our marriage hit the usual speed bumps of work, money, and family. After a while, I didn't notice them anymore. I kept driving my marital jalopy forward until one day it broke down. There may have been road signs that said Potholes Ahead, but I ignored them. Suddenly, I found myself stuck in one of those potholes on a lonely country road. Neither my marriage nor my life had any excitement. The pothole was inescapable.

Last winter, just after Christmas, the unthinkable happened. Penny and I separated. We told the kids we were taking a time out. They were familiar with the concept.

I rented the Back Bay apartment for one year, but I hung around home all the time to help the kids with their homework and to do minor repairs. I even slept over when Penny worked the eleven-to-seven shift at the hospital.

In the spring, I went off to London to present a paper at the World History Conference, and much to my daughter's delight I brought her back a Les Misérables poster from the Palace Theatre.

As soon as the ground thawed, my son and I started a long-overdue project to dig up a hunk of granite that stuck up two inches out of the dirt in front of the swing set. It turned out to be the tip of a huge boulder. We kept digging to the delight of him and his friends until we exposed this granite rock about half the size of a Volkswagen.

Every day after school, the neighborhood kids would gather around what came to be known as the "Big Hole."

"Look up the density of granite," I said.

They did and came back with an estimate of the rock's weight.

"Three tons."

No way were we going to move it. We tried the old farmer's trick of lighting a fire around it, then dousing it with cold water to watch it crack. That didn't work.

The separation didn't work either. Early in the summer, Penny and I got divorced. We promised to remain close. We had a 10-year-old daughter and an 8-year-old son to care for. They meant the world to both of us. There was never any question about that.

Divorce changed everything. Penny no longer worked nights, and she hired a handyman to fix the screen door. He also filled in the Big Hole, burying what I had so happily unearthed. We sent the kids to day camp that summer. No vacation in Chatham House for Penny and me. No vacation at all—unless you think of divorce as a permanent vacation.

If someone had said that someday she and I would divorce and that I would no longer live with my kids—.

Let's just say I wouldn't have believed them. Not in a hundred years.

When the kids went back to school, they said they no longer needed help with their homework. Penny did invite me for Thanksgiving, but it wasn't the same. She even took over my job of carving the turkey. Instead of my favorite dessert of apple pie and ice cream, she served rhubarb pie. Sweetness turned sour.

Before I left for the night, I put out the trash for collection, only to discover the Les Miz poster in a barrel.

It's what happened next that really sent me south—emotionally and physically.

Last Sunday, I called Penny. "I need to talk to you about something."

Monday morning, I stopped at—how do I even say it—Penny's house. It used to be our dream house, but the dream collapsed. The kids were in school. I was standing in our kitchen looking out the picture window to where the Big Hole used to be—she hadn't asked me to sit, so I stood there like an intruding Jehovah's Witness.

"There's nothing to discuss," she said. "The kids are coming with me to my parents' house Christmas Eve."

I know Penny. I couldn't miss her resolve. I was caught off-guard while she was almost rehearsed.

"They'll open their presents before midnight mass, and we'll go back for dinner Christmas Day, like always. It's a tradition they can't miss."

"But what about me?"

"You're not invited. We got divorced. Remember?"

That wasn't rehearsed. That was her anger seeping out. She was hurt. I was hurt, too, except my anger didn't seep out. My hurt was like a hot stove. I stayed clear of it. If I forgot and touched it, I recoiled, got away from it as fast as I could. That's why I was parked on Main Street in Chatham—a hundred miles away from Penny and no desire to go forward.

Now the car was too hot. I fixed that by shutting off the engine and cracking a window open.

All through the years of speedbumps and potholes, we tried to fix our marriage. We went to marriage counselors galore. Some of them were head cases that needed more counseling than we did. I thought with Penny's parochial school background, the priest-marriage counselor would work out. He was pretty good. One of those no-bullshit Dominicans who told it like it was.

Right in the middle of our first session, just when the priest was on a roll validating most of what I had tried to tell Penny, she turned abruptly and reached into her pocketbook. I reached in my back pocket for a hanky in case she couldn't find a tissue, but she surprised us both. She scribbled in her checkbook, ripped out a check, and gave it to him. Her parting words were, "You can both go fuck yourselves." I was really surprised, but down deep, I was proud of her. I ended up holding the hanky all the way out to my car.

There was one new-age guy who got us to try meditation. We went to the Siddha Yoga Ashram of Baba Muktananda, where the air smelled of incense, the rugs were doused with Jean Nate after-bath splash to neutralize the odor of bare-foot traffic, and the silence was broken only by heavenly tinkling bells and melodious chants. Except for sitting on the floor, it reminded me of the old Catholic church. Before we stopped going to church, our kids were baptized at folk masses with guitars and poetry. But even meditation didn't work.

In the end, nothing worked. When I was depressed, I wanted her to come to me, stroke my hair, and ask me what was wrong—instead, she mowed the lawn to ease my burden. When she was depressed, I never left her side—she wanted me to go mow the goddamn lawn.

We went to an arbiter to split up the assets so it wouldn't be a nasty divorce, and it wasn't. It was just a divorce. Divorces are nasty all by themselves.

So, there we were last Monday morning in our dream house kitchen, discussing how we were going to spend Christmas. I should say how they were going to spend Christmas—there was no "me" in the "we" anymore. She saw no way that our children could miss that family tradition to be "alone with me." I could schedule the kids on another day, like a rained-out ball game.

"But Penny, surely you don't want—I mean, can't we—"

I watched her face for some indication of sympathy, for some sign of understanding. I was staring at Mount Rushmore. How could the woman I so loved be so stone-cold cruel?

The longer her silence, the deeper my wound. I wanted to cry out, but my pride wouldn't let me. I spun around and headed out of the house. Once I started moving, an anger began roiling inside me. The pressure kept building. By the time I got behind the wheel of my car, I couldn't control it and burned rubber backing into the street. I raced away to nowhere.

The crazy thing was I didn't want my kids to miss that night with their grandparents and aunts and uncles and cousins either. It was a great tradition. Her family didn't do the feast of the seven fishes, thank God, but my mother-in-law's lasagna and chicken cacciatore were to die for. With little means, they always managed an Asti Spumante toast and red wine in crystal decanters at dinner.

None for me this year. I wasn't invited. Marriage is a package deal, and divorce is the deal breaker.

Then it occurred to me. We had another family tradition, summer at Chatham House. My kids had happy memories there. I could call Mrs. Thompson and rent the place for July and August. Penny couldn't veto that tradition. The kids would forgive my divorcing their mother, and we would recapture the fun in the life we once had. I was the phoenix of Herodotus, born again from my ashes.

I pictured a Fourth of July cookout after the parade, lazy days at the beach, lobster rolls, and dozens of walks to the Mermaid Shop and downtown for ice cream.

On Friday nights, we'd sing and dance around the bandstand. You put your left foot in, your left foot out, shake it all about. A summer of good family times—sadly without Penny—but with the kids and any of our friends who didn't see me as half of a broken tea cup.

When I got back to my apartment, I dialed sweet, old Mrs. Thompson. As the phone rang, I felt my spirits rise in anticipation, steadily upward like clicking up the first big hill of a roller coaster.

"Hello, Mrs. Thompson. This is Cliff Stone."

"Who?"

"Cliff Stone. I rent your house on the Cape every year, well not every year, not last year. But I want to rent it for July and August next summer—and if you're still interested—"

"What did you say your name was?"

"Cliff. Cliff Stone. I want to rent your house in Chatham."

"You can't, Mr. Clifton. I sold the house to a nice couple from New Jersey. They plan to retire there in a year or two."

My roller coaster was plunging downward.

"But you said you would sell it to me. Don't you remember? I wanted to buy—"

"Bye."

I sat there with the phone in my hand, aiming it around the room like a 38 special. If you move, I'll kill you.

My house!

The bitch sold my house!

I didn't know what to do. The fall semester at the university had just ended, and I wasn't due back teaching until January, same old courses: Early American History and Salem Witch Trials. Of course, true early American history ought to be about several centuries of indigenous peoples who lived here before the Europeans arrived. And the true Salem Witch Trials didn't even take place in Salem Town—they took place in the Village that is now Danvers.

Not that any of that matters. Teaching millennials and 911 babies about history is like teaching Eskimos about sunbathing.

They have no sense of it. To college kids, the assassinations of Julius Caesar, Abraham Lincoln, and JFK are all contemporaneous events from ancient times.

No wife. No kids. No Chatham House. I had nothing to do and forever to do it. I retreated into my apartment and fell into a funky depression. The slightest movement became labored, like I was suspended in Jell-O. It took hours for the clock to move by minutes. I tried getting drunk, but I don't drink. I just got a headache and the shits.

I fell deeper into the abyss. I started constructing lesson plans for my rescue. I'd starve myself for days; Penny would show up in my apartment to find my unconscious body—just in the nick of time.

That wouldn't work. She hadn't been there since she helped me pick out the apartment.

A car crash. The police would call her. "He's clinging to life. Before he lost consciousness, he said something about losing his beautiful life," or maybe "his beautiful wife." They couldn't be sure. "You'd better come now."

With no more of a plan than that, I headed south to the Cape. Traffic was light. Few people head to the cape on Sunday afternoon—fewer still in the winter. The crash never came.

I buzzed over the bridge, down the Midcape Highway, and here I was—parked on Main Street, lamenting my failed marriage, missing my kids. If I sat there any longer, I'd turn into Ebenezer Scrooge visiting Christmases past.

I stepped outside into the cold air and walked toward the ocean, facing the kind of icy December wind that burns your face and makes your eyes tear. That suited me fine. The wind would explain my tears to passers-by. Otherwise, tears betray the façade I create for the world—and for myself.

With my shoulders hunched and my woolen cap pulled down over my burning ears, I was walking toward a house where my memories lingered like ghosts of a not-so-long-ago past.

A simple plan would be to keep going past the house and hurl my body into the ocean in front of the Coast Guard station. They would see me flailing in the sea and send rescue. They would call Penny. Then she'd be sorry.

I imagined myself entering the surf, the wet weight of my clothes pulling me down. But Christ, that wind was cold. It seeped in through my collar and from the bottom of my coat. I clutched my jacket tight around my body, but the wind snaked its way up my sleeves. A sudden terror seized me—if the wind could get in, then icy water would find its way to my skin, invading my body like an army of bed bugs eating me raw. Panic grabbed my throat. I couldn't breathe.

I stopped short to regain my composure and leaned against a rickety old fence. It fell over with me on top of it. I rolled back to my feet and hustled away, colder still.

Nearly drowning was off the table. A rope was too certain. Forget about a gun. I had no means to fake my suicide and no prospects—except death by protracted depression.

It was dusk when I got to the mailbox painted with the faded numbers that marked the entry to the property. The house was set back from the road. A long dirt drive, with traces of sea shells and crushed stone from better days, led up to the imposing Mansard Victorian at the top of the rise.

The gusty wind had knocked over a real estate agent's *House for Rent* sign. I nudged it a little farther into the brush and walked in the shadows toward the house. The frozen ground crunched as I gingerly walked along the side of the drive before I ducked behind a tree. Footprints in the snow, and then poof, the Sasquatch disappeared.

Dusk turned to night as if the darkness inside me had seeped out and flooded the landscape. I became a shadow indistinguishable from my surroundings.

If I remained perfectly still, time would stop, the feelings rising inside me would stop, even the wind would stop, and I could remain in that void forever. But I couldn't. What was percolating inside me wasn't so much regret as anticipation.

The house was calling me.

Its interior was dark and foreboding. The exterior sat in the dull glow cast by a full moon that hung in the sky like an old parlor lamp with clouds for shades.

I stared at the two long windows on the left side of the first floor. They were long enough to expose a man from shin to chin, had a man been standing there, and had the shades not been pulled down. On the right side, a bow window protruded like a tugboat wheelhouse with five slender windows. The lace curtains were thick enough to shield anyone watching from inside. I had entertained myself ogling more than a few passers-by. I wondered if the spy glasses were still there.

At the center of the first floor, a magnificent carved portico with curved balustrades marked the front entry. In the faded moonlight, I could see its finish was chipping away and it was missing pieces—much as I was.

The house looked different in the dead of winter. In the summer, a thick skin of ivy crept up the first story, as if some green monster from below was trying to swallow it whole. But now, the monster's flesh was gone. Only its gnarly bones clung to the siding.

The monster's grasp reached the overhang between the first and second story. Rotting corbels shaped like G–Clefs hunched under the overhang at regular intervals around the periphery.

Many of the carved teardrops that used to attach to those corbels had fallen to the ground.

The Mansard roof curved down over the second story and met the overhang like the cover of a giant roasting pan. Pairs of gabled windows peered out through the roasting pan from each of the three upstairs bedrooms. The bedroom windows reflected black from the dark clouded sky.

Such irony. With my stocking cap pulled down tight over my head, my glasses slightly fogged, and my teardrops also fallen to the ground, that broken-down house stood, for all the world to see, as a metaphor of me.

In the years that we rented Chatham House, Penny and I slept in the large bedroom on the right, which we dubbed the Captain's Room. Our kids slept in the smaller bedrooms to its left. The middle one we called the Ocean Room because it looked directly across to the ocean; the corner room we named the Author's Room because it had a bed that was said to belong to a Chatham author who once roomed there.

Right from the beginning, I got strange but warm vibes in the Author's Room. A spooky flight of steep stairs, sized for a child's foot, led down to the kitchen. Back stairs do seem sinister, especially when the staircase near the front entrance would suffice.

The author's Victorian-era bed pleased me to no end. The large, carved headboard had raised rosewood panels, and the four pineapple-topped corner posts belonged in some exotic Polynesian plantation, not Puritan New England. The bed's well-worn mattress lay on top of an old-fashioned, exposed bed spring that gave cricket sounds when I moved.

I never felt alone in that room.

But the thing that grabbed me about that room was the locked closet at the foot of the bed, tucked under the curved Mansard eaves. On a stormy afternoon, some unseen force led me to a long-misplaced key. When I opened the skinny little door, my eyes probed the darkness of this deep chamber. It was as if I were looking into a black sea on a starless night. My eyes adjusted, and suddenly, my vision pierced the darkness.

My heart raced to my gullet. I jumped back. My head cracked the bedpost, and a carved pineapple bounced on the floor.

A woman stood motionless at the back of the closet.

I braced for her to spring forward like a tiger or some spirit that would engulf me. When nothing happened, I dared a second look. A headless form looked back. A dressmaker's form. A tool to make dresses. My rational mind was returning, and my insides were falling back to rest. Whatever was registering in my conscious mind, the ghostly image of a woman in the closet had been burned into my subconscious.

There once was a woman who used that dress form. Who might she have been? I imagined what she looked like in the flesh. I had seen a hundred drawings of pioneer women with round curls falling from their bonnets, petticoats, and boots underneath straight gingham dresses covered by white cotton aprons. But this wasn't just any woman. This was the woman who inhabited the house. A woman whose shape matched the form in the closet. A woman I would come to know. A frugal woman. A hardy woman. I felt her presence. I knew her world—one of toil and piety and obedience.

"What's your name?" I asked with my inside voice.

A gust of rain tapped against the windows. The house creaked.

"Missy" was the name I heard inside my head. I took it to be her answer. I love a responsive woman, even if it's under spooky circumstances.

I told Penny of my paranormal encounter. She dismissed it as more of my silliness. As a joke, I hung an empty picture frame with the name Missy taped to the bottom. But Penny knew I wasn't joking. I believed the house was haunted. She treated it as one of those superstitions, like it's bad luck to walk under a ladder. She didn't believe it, but she kept the closet door locked anyway.

It was in my nature to learn more about the ghost who haunted Chatham House.

And I did.

One rainy afternoon, I went to the Registry of Deeds in Plymouth to trace the history of the house ownership. I found the original owner from 1850—Captain Everett Badishall. He had built the house on one corner of farmland owned by John Hamilton.

On my way home from the Registry, I stopped at the Antiquarian Museum, using my history credentials to get into their archives. The old tax records revealed that in 1851, Captain Badishall owned the house, a cow, a fishing schooner, and 347 dollars in coin.

But, just two years before, the good captain was listed as a seaman from Nantucket who had no assets and paid no taxes. I got curious and dug a little deeper. That's when I found it.

The farmland on which the house was built belonged to the rich widow of John Hamilton. She had four unmarried daughters. The three younger ones were named Hope, Prudence, and Faith. The penniless Badishall gained his fortune when he married the eldest daughter. Her name was as close to Missy as I could expect, having had it whispered to me from a hundred-fifty years ago. Her name was Mercie!

A loud, sustained gust of wind blew from off the ocean, and I hugged the trunk of the tree to keep my balance. A tapping sound came from something loose against the house. Missy was likely watching me hide in the shadows behind the tree, and like all the dead who watch over us, she knew the pain in my heart. In a way, we were kindred spirits. She bore her pain alone in the house for so many years. All the while, the creeping vines, the crawling insects, and the nocturnal forest creatures tried to reclaim the land that was once theirs.

A light snow began to fall.

A car drove past, and I saw its headlights reflect off the beveled edges of the front door's long, oblong-shaped glass. What a door. Thick oak with a tarnished brass doorknob, also of oblong shape. I liked the feel of that elongated doorknob in my hand. The inside doorknobs were made of crystal glass—rough to the touch but ostentatious proof that this house had seen grander times.

On a normal day, I could look through the front door glass into the entry hall and all the way back to the rear kitchen. Strange how a foreboding structure would present such an open and inviting portal—*Look inside, come right in, nothing to fear here.*

Did I dare sneak up to try the front door? The outside doorknob's smooth affordance would evoke a familiar pleasure to my grasp. I longed to hold it once more. Chances were the door was locked—possibly bolted with the heavy wrought iron slider inside.

Just then, I saw a flicker of light coming from inside the house. I tiptoed across the gravel drive to get a closer look and saw a definite glow— the pulsating flicker of a flame. It could have been a small fire started by a furnace spark or an electrical malfunction. I raced toward the front door as if it were really my house and peered in through the glass with my hands shaped like binoculars.

The glow was coming from candlelight in the kitchen. A young woman placed a heavy cast iron skillet on the unlit stove. Too young to be the new owner and too modern to be the ghost from the past. She moved about, and I stood there mesmerized by her beauty—sandy blonde hair, an American-Girl doll face, a petite frame reminiscent of the form in the upstairs closet, but more contemporary curves. I imbued her with all the allure of *I Dream of Jeannie.*

Was it loneliness or desperation that drove my thoughts? For a brief moment, I took one of those faster-than-light journeys in which she and I met, fell in love, and traveled the stars until, in old age, we sat next to one another on rocking chairs, with kids and friends around us—an entire lifetime in one tiny tick of the clock.

My mother said her mother used to say, "God closes one door and opens another." The old-timers were wise. Maybe the hand of God was giving me a nudge. Meet this woman. Maybe she has a heart to match her looks. Take a shot. Wayne Gretzky said you miss 100 percent of the shots you don't take.

I raised my hand to knock on the door, not yet figuring what I was going to say when a figure emerged from the left. Another woman—not like the petite angel in the kitchen. She was my size and wore farmer's jeans over a red plaid shirt. When she spotted me, she charged in my direction and mouthed the words, "What the fuck?" She had two pigtails and a witch's crooked teeth—I remember the crooked teeth.

I signaled with my raised hand that everything was all right. She had nothing to fear from me. She called out, "Ashley!" to my dream companion in the kitchen. Ashley turned and looked straight at me. Adrenaline warmed my chest. Ashley. A perfect name. I had to remember it.

Toothy opened the door and said, "Who are you? What do you want?" She might have been hiding some blunt object behind her back. "You a cop?"

"No. My name is Cliff, Cliff Stone. I'm the new owner of this house." Where in the hell that came from, I'll never know. Maybe by using my real name, I atoned for the ownership lie.

I don't look like a cop.

"I came down to check on the property, but my real estate agent hadn't told me it was rented."

"Oh," she said.

I could see she was thinking. Me too. It was a race—between a witch and a liar.

"I didn't mean to frighten you, and I certainly don't want to disturb you."

"Do you mind waiting here a minute?" she said.

I didn't mind. It gave me time to figure out what the heck I was doing.

She went in, and I saw nothing in her hand but a fist. She whispered to Ashley, who shook her head, "No." On the second whisper, she shrugged her shoulders, "Maybe." Then she nodded a "yes" that rocked from side to side like a "yes, maybe."

The witch returned and said, "Come on in Mr.—"

"Stone."

"Yes. I'm Bobbie, and that there's Ashley." She gestured me into the kitchen, where the angel still stood next to the stove. The candlelight was bright enough to get a good look at her, and she looked good. Her skin was so smooth that I swear it reflected the candlelight. She gave me a cautious smile. If she and what's-her-name, Bobbie, were sisters, they must have had two different fathers. Maybe two different mothers, too.

"We don't know anything about the agreement you have with the real estate," Bobbie said. "We just rented it from them."

"I understand. That's fine." I'd figure out later how to explain I was the owner even though the New Jersey couple's name was likely on the lease. Maybe I could say they were my cousins, or my agents, or investors, or something. I was flying blind.

"How do you like the place?" I said looking at Ashley.

She looked at Bobbie, and Bobbie responded, "So far, so good."

"Well, I'm sure you'll love it. It's a grand old house. I especially love the contoured tin ceiling in the dining room. The walls have horsehair plaster under that flowered wallpaper. It's all turn-of-the-century." I was laying it on thick. "There's an ancient coal-fired furnace in the cellar, but it's been converted to gas." On a roll. "And don't you just love the heat that comes out of those big floor registers?

Ashley began a nod before Bobbie said, "But there ain't any heat upstairs."

"You have to leave the second-floor grates open to let the heat rise up there," I said as if I knew.

"Yeah, but we still gotta use an electric blanket."

I was stalling for time, ticking off all the things in the house that I knew. She said electric blanket, singular. Are these two together?

It occurred to me that knowing the New Jersey couple's name would help me fabricate the lie I was about to tell.

"You'll have to forgive me. I mean I trust my agent and all, but I don't know why he didn't tell me about the rental yet. Do you have a copy of the rental agreement I could look at?"

While they were discussing where they put the lease, I figured that once I had the New Jersey couple's name, I'd improvise from there. Who knows? Maybe I'd eventually end up buying the house back from them. Ashley and Bobbie would never have to know about the brief period in which I was not the owner.

Bobbie squeezed Ashley's hand and said, "I'll go get the lease. You entertain Mr. —."

"Cliff, I said. Call me Cliff." I looked over at Ashley and asked, "How long have you been here?"

"A week," she said, but at the same time, Bobbie answered, "We just arrived," then added, "We rented it a week ago, but we just arrived."

Why didn't she just go get the damn lease and leave me and Ashley alone?

She repeated, "I'll go get the lease."

Yeah. Go get the lease, why don't you?

"Watcha makin' there?" I turned on my folksy charm.

"I'm gonna cook up some fritters for supper," she said.

"I detect a little *southern* in your accent, Ashley." It's always good to use someone's name when you want them to know you're genuinely interested in them. "Where you from?"

"We came up from Florida. But I'm originally from Kentucky."

First, "we," then "I." She was definitely warming up to me. And warmth was in her nature.

"I'm Boston, born and bred. Can you tell?" Maybe she'd be interested in Boston. I could offer to show her the sights.

Bobbie returned too soon with the papers and said, "Come over here under the light."

I stepped away from Ashley and toward Bobbie, where several candles were set on the counter. It hadn't occurred to me to ask before, but I said, "Why the candlelight? Is there something wrong with the electricity?"

"You can see the lease well enough," she said, and she nodded her head in an exaggerated fashion. I was too busy planning my next move to pay much attention.

I looked at the lease in the glow of candlelight. It looked more like a brochure than a lease. A dark ring surrounded the periphery of my vision, but in that periphery, I saw Bobbie continuing to nod like an agitated horse until she finally called out, "Now!"

The dark ring collapsed into a black void. I have a vague recollection of a church bell ringing and a mallet squashing a cantaloupe.

I don't know how long I was out. A door blew open inside my head, and the outside world swooshed in. My consciousness turned on like distant fluorescents in a vast warehouse—one set banging on after another. One moment, I was in a dark chamber with no sound, and the next, everything was lit up, and the sound returned, a little muffled, like I was underwater. It was as if I was returning from a daydream, ready to resume whatever I had been doing, but I had no idea what that was.

I moved my head around to learn where the buzzing noise was coming from. I saw only hulks of shadow. The buzz was inside my ears. My legs were sprawled on a cold floor, and I was hugging a metal pipe.

Then, the pain hit—the kind of pain you get when you rise up and smash into the corner of a cabinet door you left open. It cut into the back of my head like a steel blade and throbbed like a terrified heartbeat. I couldn't rub my head. My hands were restrained.

Of course! I was on the cellar floor of that cursed house with my hands cuffed around a support column. That bitch with the crooked teeth was nodding to signal Ashley to bash me.

That a woman I so appreciated hurt me so badly was hard to accept. But was it? Didn't I love Penny? Didn't she hurt me? I don't know what hurt more, that I had been betrayed or that my skull felt like it had been cracked open.

I do know. My skull hurt more. I've always expected the women in my life to betray me. Even my mother used to say there are plenty of fish in the sea, but then never allowed me to go trolling. Once more, I was denied swimming in a sea of pretty fish. I had been lured in, hooked, yanked out, and clubbed. I was the catch—now alone in a dark cooler—a prisoner in the cellar of a haunted house . . . in Chatham's Scrabbletown . . . in the deserted winter . . . in the extreme-poverty of my pathetic life.

DESPERATE WOMEN

I heard their muffled voices upstairs, but with the wind howling outside, I couldn't quite make out their words. I stood up in the darkness and could discern in the shadows the old furnace with its heating ducts snaking to the floor registers above. I stretched my neck to press my ear against a now-cold heating duct to better hear what they were saying. Except for a slight echo, it sounded as if I were in the room with them.

"What-a we gonna do?" Ashley's meek voice seemed a little louder with worry.

"I don't know yet. Don't get all nervous; I'll figure it out." Bobbie was firmly in charge.

"They'll find out we're staying here."

"No one's gonna find out. It's the winter. Chatham is dead in the winter."

"Yeah, but he's the owner—"

"Bullshit!" Bobbie said, "He's a fuckin' liar. My grandmother's known the owner for years, and he's not her."

I had to keep a clear head if I was to get out of this situation. Bobbie's grandmother knew Mrs. Thompson. That meant Bobbie was a local or at least spent time here. She probably hadn't heard that the old woman finally sold the house. That was good. Maybe I'd convince her that I was indeed the new owner. I'd say I understood how two females alone in a house . . . hidden in the dark . . . in a deserted Chatham, could try to protect themselves from an intruder. I have a daughter myself. I wouldn't press charges.

Yeah, but what if they called the police? The police would figure out I was not the owner. Shit, then what would I do? Wait. They didn't call the police. Why not? What did Ashley say? *They're going to find out we're staying here.* That's why they didn't call the police. They're squatters. Or worse! Who the hell has handcuffs at the ready? They're guiltier than I am. I could use that. But how? I'd have to figure something before they came down to check on me.

I heard the clinking of the supper dishes going into the sink. I guess I missed dinner call. They ran the water, and I could no longer hear their conversation. They had an unconscious man in the basement, and they were calmly doing the dishes? But it wasn't "they." Ashley sounded panicked; Bobbie sounded cold and calculating—and she was calling the shots.

The water shut off. It got quiet. A tinkling noise, then quiet again. More tinkling. More quiet. They were drying the dishes and placing them on the kitchen shelves. The old-fashioned country kitchen had no cabinets.

Ashley said, "But what are we going to do with him?"

Bobbie said, "I don't know yet. I'm not sure who he is."

"You said he was a cop, but he had no badge on him. I don't think he's a cop."

"Why? Because he was sweet-talking you?"

"His wallet had pictures of his family and a Northeastern University faculty ID card. All he had in his jacket were car keys and a flip phone. Who still has a flip phone these days?"

I liked my flip phone, thank you.

"That doesn't prove anything. Not all cops have iPhones, besides, he could be working undercover. We can't take any chances. We could end up in jail."

"I told you that you never should have gotten into this business."

"Not that again. I can't deal with that now."

"But you have to deal with him now."

"No, we don't. We'll wait 'til morning."

She said it like it was a final command. A long silence followed, and then Bobbie said, "Let's go to bed."

Go to bed? They planned on leaving me there all night. What the hell?

"I'll figure it out in the morning," she said.

I heard their footsteps going up the back stairs. Open grates between the two floors allowed the heat to rise and the sound to travel between floors. I heard the squeak of the bed springs, first when one sat and then the other. They were sleeping together in the haunted, back-stairs bedroom, while the other two bedrooms remained vacant. They probably were a couple.

Even though their voices were muffled, I could still make out an occasional word or phrase. *Back to Florida*, sounded like a suggestion Bobbie made. *What about your Christmas?* sounded like Ashley's response. Maybe it was *What about your business?* I couldn't be sure.

Ashley seemed to continue asking questions, and Bobbie gave terse answers as if she were getting annoyed.

Finally, she shouted, "No!"

There was a pause, "I'm scared." Ashley's words came out with a long sob.

"I told you, I'll take care of it." The volume carried her words.

Ashley said something I couldn't hear, and Bobbie's response changed everything. "I'll kill him if I have to."

At that point, the furnace kicked on, and I couldn't hear anything more. I was locked in a dark basement, cuffed to a pole, at the mercy—Mercie, Missy, if you're here, please help me—at the mercy of two desperate women. I thought of a play my wife and I had seen at the Wellfleet Harbor Actors Theater in which some lesbian secretaries massacred a chauvinist lumberjack with a chainsaw. Wish I hadn't.

No one knew I had gone to Chatham. I wasn't due to see my kids at Christmas. I was on semester break from teaching until January sometime. No one was looking for me. I was screwed.

My best option—escape. I had the night to figure out how.

The cellar remained dark and full of shadows, except for the occasional glimpse I got when the wind blew just right and some light, either from the moon or a street lamp, found its way through a snow-flurried window.

A slight warmth radiated from the heating ducts.

I started exploring the floor with my foot, hoping to find something that I could use to break the cuffs. I made a 360-degree arc as far out as I could stretch. Nothing. I lay down on the dirty cement floor to explore a wider circle. It was cold, and it disgusted me. Still, I found nothing.

The furnace shut off again. Everything went quiet. My wrists burned from the chafing of the cuffs, and my hands felt numb. My body was shivering. My feet too were cold and numb. I stood back up and raised my leg high in the air to lean my boot on the furnace duct for warmth. The heat didn't penetrate my boot. I curled around the pole like a pretzel, unlaced my boot, and removed it. Unwinding myself from the pole, I put my wool-socked foot on the duct. It felt so good. It also pointed out a better strategy—explore above the floor, too.

I found a shelf behind the furnace duct, and my toe nudged a tool I couldn't quite reach. I removed my sock and reached my toe as far as I could onto the shelf. I could feel the metal shank of a screwdriver. Mom always said I had toes like a monkey. I shagged the screwdriver and removed it from the shelf, but my monkey toes dropped it on the floor, and it rolled out of reach. Ay, I was losing feeling in my toes.

I pretzeled my sock back on and warmed my foot on the duct. My father-in-law once explained a lazy man's fishing. "You sit by the river with a line in the water attached to your toe, and you go to sleep. When you feel a tug on the string, you decide whether or not you want to wake up to pull it in."

I removed the lace from my boot. I tied one end of the lace to the top eyelet of the boot and the other to my big toe. I maneuvered the boot onto the end of my foot and cast it in the direction of the screwdriver. When I reeled it in on my toe-rod, I heard a rattle but didn't catch the fish I was after.

The darkness. The damn darkness. If only I could have seen what I was doing.

I cast the boot again and again. The screwdriver rattled under it each time, but it took five tries to pull it in reach of my foot. I swept it across the floor to the column where my hands were cuffed.

It wasn't a screwdriver but an ice pick. I sat there trying to find leverage to break the chain between the cuffs, but nothing worked. Then I stuck it through one cuff along my wrist and tried prying it open. My wrist was going to break before the cuff gave out. I stuck the pick into the locking mechanism like a key and maneuvered it around, but nothing happened. I always wanted to know how to pick a lock but never got around to learning.

My fingers were now totally numb from the cold—maybe from the circulation being cut off at my wrists. My bare foot ached.

I put my sock back on, but the heating duct had grown cold. No more ideas were in my head.

My back ached, and I stood up to stretch. I inched the ice pick into my pants pocket in case the Sisters of Death came to do me in.

I had been at it for an hour, maybe two. Totally dejected, I leaned my forehead onto the pole that held me captive. The pole wasn't a pole. That fact had evaded my notice. The support post I was cuffed to wasn't a full-length column. It was a jack post. The top eight inches or so consisted of a rusty shaft with coarse threads that could be raised or lowered. Many years ago, it had been raised up to hold a metal plate under the house beam. A thick butterfly-wing nut at the bottom of the shaft raised and lowered it. All I had to do was turn it the right way to lower the jack, and I could slip the cuffs over the top. Just a matter of time now.

I got my two hands firmly on the wing nut and braced myself with a strong stance. Once free, I'd never tell anyone what happened. I wouldn't return to that house—to Chatham, to Cape Cod. Come summer, I'd head to the North Shore beaches of my youth—Happy Hampton, Salisbury, Newburyport.

That damn wingnut wouldn't budge in either direction. Which way was I supposed to turn it? I always got nuts and bolts mixed up. I'd turn them in the wrong direction fifty percent of the time. Make that eighty.

Okay. Had to stay cool. I ran my fingers along the screw threads to figure out the correct direction of spin. Push the right side of the butterfly and pull the left—the jack will lower. Now, all I had to do was turn the stupid thing. I gave it all the force I could muster, even suppressing a *keee-aaay* scream in my throat from my judo days. It wouldn't budge. I whacked it as best I could several times. No movement.

I was tired, hungry, cold. It was probably after midnight. I needed to rest a while before trying again. Gather my strength.

I sat lotus style on the floor—well, a lotus tied to a stake. Grow quiet, Grasshopper. Meditate. *Om nama shivaya.*

In the silence, I heard a little rustling noise. Something was definitely in the cellar with me. A field mouse probably found its way into the cellar to escape the cold. When we came to the house in the summer, we sometimes found a mouse dead in the middle of the cellar. The kids and I would scoop it up using a shovel as its funeral pyre and conduct a procession to the backyard, where we would give it a proper burial.

Each time I stirred, the noise stopped. Only when I remained silent for a while would the sound return. It was free to go wherever it wanted, yet its fear stopped it dead. If it didn't get out of there, next summer, both of us might be discovered dead in the middle of the cellar.

I jumped up and looped one handcuff over the wing nut, pressing my foot against the column for leverage. I began to see blue and brought my other foot to the column, so I was hanging out like a pole dancer in a strip club. The nut turned ever so slightly.

With my feet reset on the ground, I continued turning it. When it finally came loose from the metal plate under the beam, I spun it faster until I was able to slide my pinky between the jack and the metal plate under the beam. When I tried to maneuver the cuffs through the opening, the metal plate came loose and made a loud crash on the cement floor below.

The cuffs caught on the top of the support jack. I gave them a tug and tumbled backward onto the floor, with the whole column landing on top of me. Stunned, I lay there motionless. In the dark, I heard a creak and saw the shadow of the beam that the jack had been supporting slanted downward. It creaked again and lowered another few inches. Footsteps pounded down the back-bedroom stairway. The beam gave one last loud creak and crashed down onto the column, which hammered my leg and thigh. My leg hurt like hell, but the pain in my thigh overwhelmed me—the ice pick was stuck deep into my flesh.

"Help me!"

The cellar door opened, and the cellar light switched on like a blinding sun. Somewhere in the glare, Thelma and Louise came bounding down the stairs.

I raised my cuffed hands to shield my eyes. In my squint, I saw bare feet and flannel pajamas. Bobbie jumped down the last few stairs with a hammer cocked and ready. "You stupid shit! What have you done?" She had fire in her eyes. I scrunched my neck like a retreating turtle while my raised hands stood ready to blunt her blow. I must have looked so pathetic that she checked her swing.

Ashley was right behind, wearing bunny slippers and a tee shirt barely long enough to cover her backside. "Oh my god. Are you all right?" Squatting next to me, she pressed her hand over the blood soaking through my pants. She traced the extent of the ice pick in my thigh with measured caution, then up to the handle in my pocket. "It's not a deep wound," she said and yanked it out.

"Ay yai yai fuck," I yelled.

"Gimme that!" Bobbie ordered.

Ashley examined the ice pick and handed it to Bobbie. "That thing's filthy. We should let it bleed a minute to clean out the wound."

My blood soaked my pants and ran across her bare leg. The wound was "Cleaning out" just fine. She moved my hand over it. "Keep pressure on it." She looked me in the eye, "You're lucky it didn't go into the femoral artery."

I didn't feel lucky, except maybe that Ashley knew what a femoral artery was.

Normally, I would have thought it lucky to see her scantly covered in a nightshirt, but at this point, all I could think of was the pain. It wasn't until later that I remembered the bounce of her breasts in the shirt and the quick glimpse of darkness in her crotch. And it wasn't until much later that I internalized Ashley was half naked and Bobbie was covered up in flannel. But in that moment, when I was bleeding to death, I wasn't thinking about their sex life.

Ashley looked at Bobbie. "We gotta help him." She scanned my situation some more, "Get this off him," she said, pointing to the support column. It lay like a see-saw across my shin, with its far end pinned under the fallen beam.

Bobbie grabbed the near end of the column and lifted it. I could see the muscles in her neck bulging like a weightlifter. "Pull him free," she shouted. Ashley grabbed my belt and dragged me out.

I don't remember what I yelled, only that I was yelling. The pain in my shin rivaled that in my thigh.

Ashley stroked my face and said, "Relax, let me examine you." She replaced my hand over my bleeding thigh and said, "Keep pressure on that wound."

Her hands moved lightly down my leg until I flinched.

She looked at Bobbie and said, "His tibia's broken."

I thought I was going to pass out. I wanted to pass out. Please God, make me pass out.

She stood up and said, "I'll be right back." Then, she bolted up the cellar stairs.

I watched her backside as she ran. The higher she got, the more I saw of the two smiley faces under her white cheeks. Bobbie caught me looking. Looking was a conditioned reflex, like when I met a woman showing cleavage and had to tug my eyes toward the ceiling.

Too late. Bobbie was about to slam me, so I squinted my eyes like I was in pain. Shit, I was in pain. "You got to get me to a hospital. I won't tell. I mean, I get it. You two are squatting here—"

Her look turned deadly. I had to talk fast.

"Look, I don't belong here either. I'm not the owner. I'm here under false pretenses. I wanted to buy the house, but old lady Thompson sold it out from under me. Please, I'm hurt bad. You gotta help me."

I could see her mind working to take it all in. She said, "Ashley will take care of you. She used to be a nurse."

"Used to be?"

"She is. She's a damn good nurse."

Penny was a nurse, too. Karma.

"I need a doctor. I won't tell. I can't tell. I'm trespassing, too."

"Shut up!" she said. "I can't think with your slobbering."

"I'm not slobbering, I'm—"

"Shut up!" and she kicked my shoulder.

I may have whimpered when she did, but the fear of what she might do next made me squelch any further response.

While she paced, I checked out the cellar in the light to see what might help me. I couldn't move my torso without causing pain in my shin, so I crooked my neck and upper body as much as possible. My hand pressed my wound, which by now had stained the whole upper half of my pant leg.

The cellar was pretty much empty. The shelf where I had found the ice pick had a small toolbox. Was it empty or full? A spade shovel and an old push lawnmower leaned up against the far wall. Next to them, a sheet covered what looked like a folding bed with a mattress. An extension cord ran from a plug in the fuse box along the cellar ceiling and disappeared up into a hole in the upstairs floor.

Ashley hurried down the stairs carrying a small basket, a pillow, and a gray and black Indian blanket. She had changed into full sweats. Had she washed my blood off her leg? Had she put on underwear? When she put the basket down, I saw a bottle of water and antiseptic lying atop bandages.

She wrapped the blanket around my upper body, and then she reached into her sweats and produced a blue pill about the size of an aspirin.

"Take this," she said and took the cap off the water bottle.

"What are you doing?" Bobbie yelled. "You're not giving him my—?"

"I have to. It's all we have for the pain. I have to fix his leg."

"What are you giving me?" I meant it to sound like a demand, but it came out like a little girl's sob.

She looked at me with reassuring eyes. "Take it. It is going to be all right."

HEAVEN AND HELL

I swallowed the blue pill. Ashley took back the bottle and handed it to Bobbie. Somehow, their roles had gotten reversed. Ashley was in charge, and Bobbie was her assistant.

She placed the pillow under my head and asked, "How's that?"

"Great," I said.

She touched my face and said, "You're going to fall asleep now, and I'm going to fix your leg."

"You know how?"

"I do."

I trusted her even though she had clobbered me with a frying pan. I can't blame her for that. She thought I was a threat, and Bobbie told her to do it. Still, she did it. What kind of a person hits another person so hard that they're knocked unconscious? The kind of person who could poison me with a pill and a smile on her face.

But it was too late now. She was running things—not only with Bobbie but also with me. The kindness in her eyes and the softness in her face showed only concern. It was the look I so wanted when I asked Penny about Christmas.

I didn't fall asleep. I was looking up at Ashley with the cellar light shining in my eyes. It reminded me of birthday candles on a cake. I closed my eyes to wish. Euphoria filled my brain and my body. What should I wish for? I opened my eyes, and Ashley was staring back at me.

I closed them again, and my spine began to buzz as if a thousand honey bees were filling my insides with warm nectar.

Ashley rocked me toward her and tucked the blanket under the length of my body. Then she covered me and rolled me away, tucking the blanket under my other side. I was wrapped in a tight cocoon with something propping me up. Was it the bulk of the blanket, or was she lying beside me? I was too groggy to figure it out.

What I did perceive was Ashley's hands grasping me here and there. I felt a dull ache in my groin when her hand pressed against my icepick wound. It was like the ache I had when Penny and I were first married, and she had Wednesdays off. I willed Penny out of the slow-motion vortex where Ashley and I spun.

Ashley removed my trousers, and a comedian made a joke: sex is like real estate—popular because it's centrally located. The soundtrack filled with laughter. The vortex filled with pleasure. Tantric. Full-body.

The pain in my broken leg came and went as if it were actually in someone else's leg, and the pain was being telepathically sent to me—attenuated and after the fact. Each twinge of pain turned into a surge of pleasure, and the pleasure continued to expand, spilling into the vortex in which she and I were floating. The vortex dissipated, and everything became calm. I lost all sense of time or place, reveling in the bliss.

We floated in a cloud, between billowy sheets, on a mattress of soft moss and silky-green tropical leaves. A purple river flowed alongside. Ashley and I had become Adam and Eve in the Garden of Eden—beyond sexual—part of creation itself.

In the distance, we watched a ruby sunset—her warm body cuddled next to mine—and we surrendered to sleep.

On waking, I stretched my right arm over my head. It felt good that my hands were no longer shackled together. I reached for Ashley and discovered that my left arm was somehow restrained. Ashley wasn't there.

No one was there.

Instead of sunshine and lush green gardens, everything was gray and dirty—hand-hewn beams and old floorboards above me, cement walls around me. I was still in the cellar, but daylight had chased away the dark. It was already the next day. Monday, I figured, although there was no reason for figuring it. I didn't have to be anywhere. First time I wished I had a faculty meeting—maybe someone would come looking for me. No, they wouldn't. I frequently missed faculty meetings. No one at school was looking for me. Penny and the kids weren't.

Get real.

I was lying not on a bed of leaf-covered moss but on the moldy mattress of the folding bed I had seen earlier. My left wrist was cuffed to the frame. No billowing, white sheets, no warm body against mine. A sheet and an electric blanket covered me. The blanket was plugged into an orange extension cord coming from the other side of the cellar. I had gone from the Garden of Eden to the Waiting Room of Hell.

I lifted the sheet to see that my pants were gone. The ice pick wound in my thigh was covered with a large gauze patch and secured with ample strips of white tape. Pink panties. I was wearing pink panties. It looked like a speedo on the statue of a Greek God that had its penis chopped off by the nuns.

My right leg was braced by two boards that ran from my thigh to the bottom of my foot. They were bound together in three places with rounds of duct tape. My winter boot had been replaced by a sneaker, hog-tied to the boards with the laces. The tip of the sneaker and the tip of my sock had been cut off, so my toes were exposed.

The boot on my other foot was also gone, but the wool sock remained.

I needed to pee. Real bad.

"Hello! Is anyone up there? I need help."

At first, I didn't hear a response, but when I yelled a second time, I heard footsteps scurrying across the floor. It was Ashley who hurried down the stairs.

"Are you awake?"

"I have to pee."

She reached down beside the bed and produced a pewter pitcher. It was the one that Penny had used to make lemonade in the summer.

My bladder was about to bust, but I tried not to show it. "Thank you," I said.

"Are you hungry? I made you some soup."

"I could use some soup." My face must have been distorted because I was holding my sphincter muscles tense.

"I'll be right back with it."

As soon as she got to the stairs, I hit that pitcher with a deluge. I wasn't sure if it was going to be big enough, but eventually laid it carefully next to the bed so as not to spill it.

When Ashley returned with a cup of soup, she looked down at me. "Don't move. Here, drink some soup."

"Wait," I said, "can you tell me what's happening?"

"What do you remember?"

"I had an accident. You gave me a pill."

"You broke your leg, and I set it."

She raised the cup and maneuvered the straw toward my lips, but I resisted. "How do you know it's even broken? Don't we need an X-ray?"

I got a whiff of the soup when she pulled it away. "It's broken all right. All blue and swollen. And you were in a lot of pain."

"I need medical attention."

"I fixed you up last night. It's a simple fracture. Nothing's out of place. Stable. You'll be okay for a couple of days."

"A couple of days?"

"Yeah, Bobbie is off doing business. She'll be done by tomorrow, and you need to recover a bit before we move you.

"What then?"

"We're leaving. I think Bobbie's gonna drop you off at the Cape Cod Hospital or something."

It was the "or something" that worried me.

"You know, I just want to get home to my family. We're supposed to go somewhere Thursday—no Friday." I accepted the couple of days, added one day at the hospital, and made up the Friday thing as insurance. My brain was functioning again. "I won't tell anyone. I can't."

"I know. Bobbie told me. You'll be all right until then. Nothing bad's gonna happen to you."

"I don't want to contradict you," I gave her a slight smirk, "but I'm locked in a cellar with a broken leg. Isn't that already bad?"

She almost smiled, then she said, "I'm sorry . . . I mean . . . Let's not let the soup get cold." She put a straw in my mouth, and I sucked in some warm broth. It felt really good—not as good as filling that pitcher and certainly nowhere near as good as the sex I didn't have. I kept sucking down the soup, telling her how good it was, and thanking her until the cup was empty.

"My leg. It hurts."

She felt my forehead. "You need to rest now." Her hand stroked downward to rest on my eyelids. I breathed in the scent of her hands. It reminded me of some herb I couldn't quite place.

"I'm still in a lot of pain. You gotta help me."

"It'll only be another day.

"I don't know if I can last that long. It hurts too much." Now that I said it, it hurt even more. Even if it was going to be one day, I wouldn't mind taking another joy ride on whatever it was that Ashley gave me. "Can you give me something?"

"Bobbie says I can't give you any more of the stuff I gave you."

She didn't name the drug, but she's a nurse. She knew the name.

I can give you some Tylenol. That will help the pain."

"Tylenol! No, that won't touch it. Don't you have more of those blue pills?"

"Yeah, but Bobbie said no."

"Please. Get me a couple of those. I won't tell."

Just then, we heard an upstairs door slam and the heavy footsteps of someone walking across the floor.

"Ashley!" It was Bobbie's voice, loud and demanding. Angry.

Ashley whispered to me, "Hang in there, I'll talk to Bobbie. We'll get you something."

She ran upstairs and left the cellar door open. I heard her say, "I was taking care of business."

"My business needs takin' care of."

"I just fed him some soup."

"We got bigger problems than soup."

It was one of those quiet December days when the air outside was cold and still. No wind whistling, no icy precipitation crackling against the windows. Bobbie's voice could be heard through the open cellar door as well as propagating down through the heating ducts. I needed only to raise my head out of the muffling pocket of my pillow.

"We're in deep shit," she said.

"I know. He's still in a lot of pain."

"Who?"

"Cliff . . . Cliff Stone."

"Screw him! He's the least of our problems. I've got big problems."

What could be a bigger problem than me with a broken leg in the cellar? I was hoping it was something immediate. Maybe a heart attack creeping up her left arm as she spoke.

"What's the matter?" Ashley asked.

"Carlos didn't show up."

"Carlos, your distributor?"

"More than my distributor. Our ticket out of here."

It appeared that Ashley knew how Bobbie was going to get rid of the drugs but still was not part of the process.

"I drove all the way down to Truro because he wouldn't deal over the phone. Brought him these samples. If he liked them, he would buy the whole kit and a caboodle. Then we could get our money and get the hell out of here."

"Can I have one of those blue pills for him?"

"Who?"

"Cliff. The guy in the basement."

"Jesus, Ashley! We just lost a hundred-thousand-dollar sale, and you're worried about numb nuts in the basement?"

"He's in a lot of pain."

"He's in pain? Shit, we needed that money. I owe 50 thousand to the guys in Florida. If I don't get back there in a week and pay them, they'll come looking for me. Then you'll see what real pain is."

"But you said it was going to be easy, like last year. What happened?"

"I don't know what happened. Carlos is gone. His place was all locked up. His neighbors said they haven't seen him for a few days."

"Maybe he'll be back soon."

"Or maybe he's in jail, or on the lam, or maybe he's dead. I don't know. We can't afford to wait."

"What are we gonna do?"

"I'll think of something."

"How?"

"Don't push me. I've been thinking about it all the way back. I have a plan."

"What plan?"

"I told you. Don't push me."

"I'm not pushing. You said you have a plan. Do you? What is it?"

"Tomorrow."

It sounded like Bobbie was stalling.

"Tomorrow what?"

"Tomorrow, I'll go to Hyannis. I have some contacts there."

There was a silence. Did it mean she believed Bobbie, or did it mean she didn't?"

"Okay. Tomorrow you go to Hyannis, but what about . . . you know, in the cellar."

Smart. She avoided using my name again. It seemed to trigger Bobbie.

"Him? I haven't figured that yet. First things first. One thing I do know, we can't just leave him at the hospital. Sure as shittin', he'll call the cops."

I was already planning what I'd tell the police. *I knocked on the door to inquire about renting the house, and she clobbered me.*

"No. I don't think he will." Ashley said.

"Grow up, Ash."

"No, really. I've been talking to him. He just wants to go home to his family. They have something to do or someplace to be on Friday."

"I don't want you talking to him.

"I gotta talk to him. To feed him. To take care of his wound."

"You don't need to talk to him. You can't trust him. He'll give you a line of bullshit. You know how gullible you are."

"I'm not gull—."

"Your only job is to make sure that idiot doesn't go anywhere."

"He's not goin' anywhere. He's in a lot of pain. It could be that I didn't set his leg just right. I should give him another Fentanyl pill."

"What? No! You can't do that. We need that stuff."

"You can spare a few. You got like a thousand of them."

"They're not for him. That's my business."

"But he's in a lot of pain."

"You want me to go down there and put him out of his misery?"

It didn't sound to me like I was going to get any more medication. At the time, I hadn't heard about Fentanyl. What a killer it was. All I knew was that when I took it, I felt great, and right now, my leg was throbbing. An infection was even establishing little outposts in my wound.

The light started to fade. It was already dusk. I decided to stay quiet, fearful of how Bobbie would react to even the slightest peep out of me. My only hope was that Ashley wouldn't forget about me.

Bobbie said, "I gotta put these samples away," and she bounded up the stairs.

Ashley slipped down into the cellar with four Tylenol and a glass of water. "Here," she said, "take these for now. I'll get you more later."

"Thanks, Ashley. I don't know what I'd do without you here."

"Gotta go," and she ran up the stairs.

I gave a whisper-shout, "Can you turn the cellar light on?"

"Sure," she said and flipped the switch.

The arm cuffed to the bed frame was aching, so I tried to turn and snuggle it under the electric blanket. My leg shot a sharp pain, and I jumped back. I could feel the pull in my wound. To make matters worse, my sinuses were filling up, and my eyes were burning. The mold in the mattress was bringing on my allergies. I was so miserable. Things couldn't get worse.

And then they did.

Bobbie came down the stairs without Ashley. She had a threatening look in her eye. She said, "I want no trouble from you. You try to get away, and so help me, I'll tie you up in the backyard and leave you for the coyotes."

"I understand," I said in my most conciliatory voice, "but you have to get me out of this cellar. My allergies are popping from the mold, and by the morning, I could be a basket case." She didn't seem to react negatively, so I added, "And I need painkillers badly." I moaned that last statement out.

She said, "I'll talk to Ashley." Her demeanor was almost pleasant. My plea must have hit a resonant chord in her heart. I no longer feared being eaten by coyotes in the cold.

"Thank you, Bobbie." I used her name to encourage our new bond, much as I had with Ashley—although wishing a different outcome.

She went upstairs and shut the cellar light.

"No, don't shut—" It was too late. She had left me in the dark again.

I could hear her and Ashley discussing the painkillers, but the furnace kicked on, and I couldn't quite make out the words. I had no choice but to wait to find out what they decided.

With the hum of the furnace, the cold, the aches in my body, and my eyes all watery and red, I fell off to sleep. I woke to the silence of the furnace being off. I heard nothing from the floor above me. The only sound I heard was the labored breathing from my open mouth—my sinuses were totally blocked.

I again noticed the tick of a dried-up leaf stirring in the cellar. The mouse was back. I listened carefully this time, remaining still through a long silence. I heard it again. It sounded like it came from under the cot.

"Shoo!" It could go play in another part of the cellar. To ensure it scurried away, I managed a strong wiggle that made the bed bump slightly sideways.

Something hit my cheek as if someone had shot an elastic band from across the room. Whatever exclamation was about to come out of my mouth never materialized because this time the elastic landed in my mouth, and it took me a microsecond to realize it was alive with prickly legs. I spit its crispy body out and started yelling loudly. "Help! Help! Help!"

I kept yelling until the cellar light came back on, and I saw huge black bugs jumping to the corners of the room. Ashley and Bobbie found me thrashing in the bed. The heating blanket and sheet had been kicked off. My speedo slipped into my crotch. Pain shot up and down my leg. I was in the middle of a full-monty panic attack.

"What's the matter with you?" were the first words out of Bobbie's mouth.

I managed, "A cockroach just landed in my mouth." I spit and thrashed, struggling against the handcuff.

She looked around and said, "It's just a spider cricket. They're all over the Cape."

I kept thrashing. "I can't stay here. I'm freezing. I'm allergic. It's filthy. I can't stay here. I can't."

Ashley said, "We've got to help him."

"How?"

She whispered to Bobbie, "Let's move him upstairs."

Bobbie looked up as if she were saying, *God help me in my troubles.* She closed her eyes and shook her head. Ashley rubbed her shoulder, and Bobbie unlocked the handcuff from the bed.

The relief to my arm helped me to stop whining. I started to tell her that we'd all be better off if I were upstairs.

"Shut up!" she said.

"Stay calm," was Ashley's caution. Everything would be all right. She took the sheet from the floor and folded it up. I took the opportunity to readjust my panties. I didn't like Bobbie seeing my private parts.

Ashley moved my legs to the edge of the bed while Bobbie pulled me into a sitting position. I screamed in pain. Bobbie stepped back and Ashley half-hugged me as she lowered me back to a prone position. Then, she gently moved my legs back to the center of the bed. She used her hands to wipe the tears from my eyes.

"Go get him one of the pills," she said with no hesitation. A command. No room for argument.

Bobbie gave none. She ran up two flights of stairs and came down with a blue pill and a glass of water.

I questioned nothing, partly because Ashley was fully in charge of both Bobbie and me and partly because I wanted another taste of that magic blue pill. I gulped it and the water down. "Get me out of here," I was almost weeping.

"It's all right," Ashley said. "Just relax. Breathe. Slow. That's it. In and out. In and out."

It took a while, but I didn't mind the wait. I was out of the darkness. Ashley's hand was on my chest, encouraging slower breathing. Bobbie was doing something with her boot—maybe sweeping away a spider cricket. I didn't care.

Eventually, another wave of euphoria came over me. I was impervious to whatever was going on around me. I drifted off into never-never land where everything existed, but nothing had a name. I heard Ashley's voice say, "Up." She and I careened through space like we were on a long Disney ride wrapped in a warm cocoon, floating this way and that. At the end of the ride, we landed on a soft bed in a deserted field where only the hum of cicadas and the trill of crickets serenaded us, and we settled into a serene sleep—untroubled by the world.

A QUIET VOICE

I reached out. Both my hands were now free, but left or right, she wasn't there. I heard a familiar squeaking noise. A mouse? A pig? I tried to turn my body, and a pain in my leg caused my hips to lurch upwards. I came down to a louder squeak and bounced to an attenuated one. I opened my eyes.

Pink-flowered wallpaper covered the walls. A heavy quilt covered my body all the way to the foot of the bed between two pineapple-topped bedposts. Behind me was a carved headboard. I was in the Author's Room, the back-stairs bedroom where I first encountered Missy.

One window faced the ocean; the other sat over the driveway that ran from the street along the side of the house and looped in the back toward the hundred-foot-long shed that stretched behind the house to the wood line. The window shades were pulled down against the daylight. The room was dark, but not as dark as the cellar—more like a movie theater with courtesy lights. It must have been Tuesday.

A set of handcuffs was around the bedpost by my feet. I removed the quilt to see that my good leg had another set around my ankle. The set attached to the bedpost and the one attached to my ankle were linked by a bicycle lock cable with an integral combination lock. I was on a two-foot leash

Everything else in the room was pretty much as I remembered it. The closet door was closed. I whispered, "Missy, if you're in there, I could use you now."

Did I expect a response?

I hadn't expected one that rainy day so many summers ago when I asked her name. But I got the definite answer: "Missy." It wasn't so much a sound I heard as it was a thought impressed into my mind—the way you would expect a ghost to communicate.

Maybe she said "Mercie," but I like to think she said "Missy," as if that was what her mother and sisters called her. I called her Missy as a term of endearment during all those rainy afternoon naps I took in the back-stairs bedroom. She never seemed to mind.

I told her I knew her story. She was a colonial-times girl who had to do what her mother commanded, even if it was marrying her off to a sailor who—up to that time—had not found his fortune at sea or in the taverns but likely cleaned himself up for a Sunday service to nab a rich urchin who would mend his clothes, keep his house, and satisfy his out-at-sea-too-long desires.

The Town records said she lost her only son to the "fever" when he was two. Within a year, the Captain was also lost at sea. No record existed of his body ever washing ashore, and yet a stone with his name marked an empty grave in the Seaside Cemetery. She lived the rest of her adult life alone in that house, and her body was buried next to that empty grave.

Sometimes, she and I often had late-night talks. I told her I understood her grief. I believed she understood mine.

Missy was the indomitable spirit of Chatham House. She waited within its walls for the return of her husband from sea, and she often lingered in her son's back-stairs bedroom.

So, here I was, a captive in that back-stairs bedroom.

Whether I expected a response or not, I again whispered, "Missy, if you're in there, I could use you now."

I closed my eyes, like when you make a birthday wish, and I waited.

"Are you in pain?" A quiet voice, but a voice nonetheless. A voice so sweet that it compelled me to open my eyes.

Ashley hovered over me. She had her hair down. Last time I saw her in the cellar, it was pulled back in a teenage ponytail with Olivia-Newton-John-in-*Grease* bangs. Now, she was Marilyn Monroe in *Some Like It Hot*.

"Is it tomorrow?" I asked, as if I had any sense of time.

"It is. It's Tuesday," she said. "You had a peaceful night."

"Yeah, that blue pill you gave me really did the trick. What was it?"

"Can I get you some breakfast, Cliff?" She remembered my name.

"Yeah, that would be great, Ashley." I put whipped cream on the Ashley.

"Scrambled eggs, coffee, cream and sugar, toast—okay?"

"Great!"

She started to leave.

"Ash?" I pushed the intimacy slightly forward, "Thanks. I don't know what I'd do if you weren't here."

That was a dumb thing to say. If Ashley—Ash, she didn't balk at the diminutive—If Ash hadn't been there, I probably wouldn't have ended up in the cellar. Still, there was an ounce of sincerity buried in my comment, and it landed well. She gave me a big smile before she headed down those skinny little stairs to the kitchen.

There wasn't much else I could do. Ashley was my only hope. I had to convince her to let me go. She was more of a nurse than a drug dealer. Somehow, she had gotten involved with Bobbie, and now she was in over her head. I had to convince her she was too sweet a girl to be involved in a drug deal. Maybe I could convince her to get out.

When she returned with my breakfast, I said, "Can you stay with me while I eat? Take my mind off the pain?"

I could see her weighing the pros and cons in her mind. "Okay, but just while you eat."

She pulled up the antique chair with the cane backing and seat, the same chair I used to put my son's clothes on when I put him to bed at night. But nothing I ever put on that chair made it look as good as it did with her sitting on it.

I took a slow sip of coffee.

"You know I know," I said.

"Know what?"

"That you two don't belong here, in this house, any more than I do. That's true, isn't it?"

She hesitated.

"No," she said. "I mean, Bobbie knows this house. She knows the woman who owns it."

She was uneasy. She didn't want to lie to me, but she was afraid to tell me the truth. I thought she might bolt. I changed the subject.

"You told me you're from Alabama?"

"Kentucky."

Damn! I had to pay more attention.

"You're not eating your breakfast."

The toast had butter and jam on it. There wasn't much else to do but eat a few mouthfuls and wash them down with sips of coffee.

"How did you end up with Bobbie? I hope you don't mind my asking. I mean, she seems like she'd be a nice person when she wasn't so stressed."

"She is. I met her when I came to Cape Cod on vacation."

"You two are a couple?"

Again, she hesitated. This time, it was a simple question, but I couldn't tell if she didn't want to tell me because she was embarrassed or she didn't want me to think she was taken. She may have nodded yes, or was her head crooked slightly to a maybe? I took it to be a yes.

"That's cool," I said. I wanted her to not feel threatened, to keep talking. I took a few more bites of egg and toast and the smallest sip of coffee I could. "What was it like growing up in Kentucky?"

"Oh, you don't want to hear that."

"Sure, I do. I'm guessing you were raised as a Southern Belle."

"No, just the opposite. I was a Tomboy. I used to like to climb trees 'n' go fishing. My two sisters were the Southern Belles. My Daddy used to joke he had three kids, two girls and me."

"Did you ever like boys—when you were younger?"

"Oh yes, I liked them all right. We all did. My older sister married a real southern gentleman, but Corrine, the middle one, got pregnant in high school, and Daddy had a real shotgun wedding. Then Mama died, and Daddy—."

"I'm sorry to hear about your mother. That must have been hard for you."

She looked down. I thought I saw a tear forming in her eye.

"Yeah, I sure missed Mama." She took a long time with a thought inside. I remained quiet. "That's when Daddy changed."

"How?" I could see she was looking at my dish, so I munched some toast with a little scrambled egg swept on.

"He wouldn't let me go anywhere without giving my date the third degree. All the boys knew about my sister and his shotgun in the closet, so they stopped calling. Then, Daddy stopped letting me go anywhere at all."

"Ouch."

"Yeah. I kinda had a breakdown. That's when my aunt took me on vacation to Cape Cod."

"I'll bet that's when you met Bobbie?"

"Yup. She was cutting the lawn at the place we stayed. Bobbie's really very sweet. I know it doesn't seem that way to you right now, but she's got a big heart. And she's funny, too. She took me under wing. Saved me, really."

I was running out of eggs and toast to keep the conversation going, so I took smaller sips of coffee.

"You been together since?"

"No. I went back to Kentucky. Finished high school. Went to nursing school near my house. We corresponded all the time, and she even came down to visit one time. Helped Daddy with all kinds of chores around the farm. He loved her at first."

"What happened?"

"I went on Spring Break to Ft. Lauderdale, and Bobbie came down, too. She was still living with her grandmother then. We loved Florida. Said we'd love to move there someday.

"And your father?"

"Well, he didn't exactly know. In my last year of nursing school, Bobbie moved down to Kentucky, and she started showing up all the time. That's when Daddy went a little crazy. He threw her out of the house and told her to never come back."

"That's tough. What did you do?"

"I couldn't do much. I finished nursing school and got a job at the hospital. I dated a few boys for Daddy's sake, but I snuck out with Bobbie whenever I could."

"You had your sisters?"

"Not really. Karen, my older one, she was appalled at the whole thing. And Corrine, I'll never understand. She had four kids by then and was in this miserable marriage with Donny, her husband, and she tried to fix me up with Donny's younger brother, who was more of a bum than Donny."

"Jeez, Ashley, that's terrible." By this time, a tear had appeared in her eye. I watched it roll down her cheek and wiped it off just as her hand came up to do the same.

She straightened her back.

"So what happened with your father?"

"Daddy died. Karen sold the farm and put my third in trust for when I got married."

"Married?"

"Yes. It's even worded in the trust that it has to be to a boy."

"I'm sorry. That must have been really hard for you—losing your father and having your sister turn on you like that."

"It was. That's when Bobbie and I moved to Florida."

"That was a bold move. Took a lot of courage. Good for you."

"Not so good."

"Why not?"

"Bobbie had trouble finding work. She was doing landscaping like when she was on Cape Cod, but with all the Cuban workers getting low wages, she couldn't make much money—and she was killing herself in the hot sun."

"Did you get a job?"

"I did, in the hospital, but it all went wrong."

"Tell me about it."

"Maybe another time."

I tried to get her to tell me more, but I could see she was nervous about spending that much time with me.

She said, "You done eating? I'll bring the tray downstairs."

She was clearing it. I had to think fast.

"Ashley, I have to go to the bathroom."

She looked down at the pewter pitcher next to the bed.

"No, that won't do," I said.

She put the tray down on the dresser and said, "Okay, but you can't put any weight on your leg." She looked at a piece of paper in her pocket and then unlocked the bike lock. "You'll have to lean on me."

It appeared she had thought it all through. She got me out of bed and wrapped my arm over her shoulder.

"Where's Bobbie," I asked.

"She's out on business."

"Yeah, I heard that her buyer evaporated."

She looked at me as if to ask *how did you know that?*

"I said, "I could hear from the back stairs."

"Oh."

That seemed to satisfy her.

"Now, put your weight on me, not on your leg."

We started hop-stepping toward the bathroom. I felt some pain but didn't complain. The last thing I wanted her to do was to improvise a bed pan out of a serving bowl. We had to go through the Ocean Room to get to the corridor that led from the front stairs, past the Captain's Room, to the bathroom in the rear.

"Does she have another buyer?"

"Not yet, but Bobbie knows a lot of people around here. She'll find someone else to buy the merchandise."

She stuttered a bit, tripped over the word merchandise. When we passed through the Ocean Room, where they slept last night, I saw that all their stuff was in there. The Captain's Room was unused, except I noticed a lone duffel bag in the corner.

We got to the bathroom. It was the size of a telephone booth, and you had to step up to enter because the floor was raised to retrofit the plumbing. When the house was built in 1850, Thomas Crapper had just invented the flush toilet, and most houses still had outhouses. Upstairs bathrooms were a 20th-century invention.

I did my business in the bathroom and she helped me back to the Author's Room. This time, I let out a couple of squeals from the pain. By time she locked me up again, I was sweating profusely.

"How's the pain?" she asked.

Now that I was back in bed, it wasn't that bad.

"It's pretty bad," I said. "Can I have another blue pill?" I figured if I was going to be there another day, I might as well take another trip to never-never land. I figured that stuff could be addictive, but I thought one more would get me through the day, and then I could go back to my sober life.

"Bobbie doesn't want me to give it to you."

"Why not?"

"I don't know. She has a lot of them, but—"

"It's okay." I didn't want to push her. She was clearly afraid of Bobbie. I was, too. I decided to take a different tack.

"Can you stay a little longer? Talking helps keep the pain off my mind."

"I suppose," she said, but this time she didn't sound reluctant. Maybe thinking about leaving made her want to stay more. They have a name for that in psychology, but I forgot what it is. I think it did her good talking with me. She sat back down.

This was my opportunity. I had shown her empathy—it was easy to do. Besides being so pretty, she was a precious soul. All I needed to do was get her to feel something—anything—for me, and maybe she'd let me go before Bobbie got back. I wasn't sure how. My car was still parked back near the Squire. I'd worry about that later.

"You know, I need to get out of here. I need to get back to my family. Well, to my kids. My wife and I are no longer together." Might as well put that on the table and see if she picked it up.

"I'm so sorry."

Wasn't sure what she was sorry for. That I needed to get out of there, that I had to get back to my kids, or that Penny and I had split up. I have to stop using compound sentences.

"My wife was a nurse too. I mean she still is . . . a nurse, not my wife. She was student nurse of the year her senior year. What can I say? I have a thing for nurses."

"You like blood and bedpans?" She had a sly smile on her face.

"You're not only beautiful, but you're funny too."

She took the compliment well.

"Your kids?"

"A girl 10, and a boy 8. Love them to pieces. I guess I still love my wife, too. I never expected I would end up divorced. I mean, Penny and I were sweethearts since college days. If love is real, it never ends. What ends is your ability to live with someone you love."

I could see her thinking that one over—you never stop loving; just can't be together anymore. She thought she loved Bobbie. Someone who understood her, took care of her–when her father and sisters didn't, when her mother was gone. But she didn't belong in this life. Maybe she was thinking she couldn't stay in the relationship anymore.

"What happened with your wife?"

She was interested.

"I'm not sure I know. My mother got cancer. Her father had a heart attack. The kids were sick a lot. I worked days. She worked nights. Nothing bad, like an affair or anything happened. We were living two different lives. It was more than that. She seemed angry all the time. I didn't feel loved or cared for as I had in past years."

Different lives. Angry. She couldn't miss the parallels.

"Then, when it came to Christmas, she didn't want me to see my kids." I could see Ashley's expression change to sympathy. "That's when I came down here. This place, this house." I turned my body towards her and winced. "It's the last time I was happy."

My sad story was working. She had empathy written all over her face. But then, my sad story was indeed sad.

"So, you're not going to see them on Christmas?"

I hung my head down, squeezing every last bit of sympathy I could from her. "No, I won't."

"What about Friday?" she asked.

"Friday?" I rolled Friday around in my head.

"You said you had something to do with your wife and kids on Friday."

I had to think fast. "Well, I lied a little. Penny has an uncle who died, and the funeral is Friday. The truth is we weren't going together, but I was hoping to see them there." The truth train had long since left the station.

"Are they expecting you?"

"Probably not." The truth was coming around the bend.

"Well, maybe that's for the best."

"Why's that?"

"If no one is expecting to see you, then being here a few more days or the rest of the week, won't make any difference."

I didn't see that coming. I had to say something to get us off that track and back on the track of getting out of there.

"Excuse me for saying this, Ashley, but you don't seem happy here."

She took a deep breath—the way someone does when they take a long puff on a cigarette before answering a question.

"We live in Florida. We're up here only because Bobbie has business to do."

It was easy to figure. Florida, the drug capital of the East Coast, and Cape Cod, the haven of partying college kids and working poor serving the rich. Supply and demand. I got an A in economics, but I decided to become a historian because I love poverty.

I placed my hand over hers. "I know you're a good person. I can tell."

"Thank you," she said. "I should go now." She pulled her hand loose from mine, not in an abrupt way, more casual, like it was okay where it was but might not be if it stayed.

I took her hand again. "But I have to ask you something else, please."

She seemed open.

"What?"

"You've got to let me go. I won't make trouble for you—God knows you've had enough trouble in your life. I just need to get some medical care, get home, and figure out a way to put my life back together. Ash, you have to let me go right now."

She glanced at the ankle lock. For a moment, I thought she might unlock it and set me free. Instead, she listed to the right like she was going to fall off the chair. She rose to her feet and made a quick loop.

When she faced me again, her countenance had changed. Her eyes were bulging, and her lips were pursed tight, holding back whatever emotion was in there. I didn't know whether she felt bad that she couldn't let me go or if she was afraid of what would happen to her if she did. Either way, I knew who she was afraid of. A deluge of tears came out.

She grabbed the breakfast tray and ran down the back stairs.

The crash of dishes and thump of her body on the stairs said she slipped halfway down.

"Are you all right, Ashley!" I yelled.

The tears turned into loud weeping. She sent her answer into the ether. "No, I'm not all right. I'm never all right."

I could hear Ashley cleaning up the broken dishes. After that, stone silence. I couldn't even tell which room she was in. Time went by. I don't know how much. It seemed like forever. I was getting hungry again when I heard her in the kitchen.

She brought up a tray with a cheese sandwich and stood her distance.

"Look, Cliff, I would like to let you go now, but I just can't. I can't do that to Bobbie. She's got big problems right now, and I can't give her any more time to think about them. Please don't ask me again. Bobbie will let you go when she finishes her business. I'm sure of it."

It's okay, Ashley. Right now, I'm more concerned about you. Did you get hurt?"

"I'm all right. I've had worse."

"Sit a minute. I won't bite. Promise."

I was surprised at how willingly she did.

"How's the pain?" she asked.

"I'm all right," I added with a little bit of affect. "But I haven't had worse."

We both laughed at that.

"So, tell me. What's going on that has you so worried."

"Bobbie. She has to find another buyer fast. We were only supposed to be here for a day or two before driving back to Florida. We have to get back. She owes a lot of money to some bad people."

"This doesn't sound like you, or from what you tell me, Bobbie even. How did you get into this mess?"

"It's my fault really. I got in a lot of trouble, and Bobbie had to get us out of it."

"What happened?" I said it softly, sympathetically, like an old friend trying to help.

"It's complicated. Let's just say I lost my job, and Bobbie lost hers because of it. We couldn't pay our rent, and we were out on the street. I just wanted to run away where no one knew us."

"It was that bad?"

"Yeah, it was bad."

"You don't have to tell me if you don't want to."

She looked like a big conflict was going on inside her head. I didn't want to give her any more consternation.

"What did you end up doing?" I asked

"Bobbie took me to Tampa, Ybor City, really. She had to take drastic action for us to survive."

"I'm guessing what that drastic action was."

"She came up with the idea of our coming up to the Cape once a year and making a lot of money in one transaction."

"And?"

"She made a contact here that would pay double the price of stuff she could get in Ybor City."

"Sounds desperate . . . and smart. How did she pull it off?"

"She borrowed some money on the street and used that money to buy the stuff."

"That sounds pretty risky."

"I guess, but it was supposed to be a sure thing. And it worked so well last year that this year, she borrowed a lot more. She was going to make enough to give us a fresh start—maybe out west."

"Out west?"

"Yeah, I always wanted to go to California. We could start over."

"Now I understand. And I came along and screwed everything up."

"No, it wasn't you. It was this guy, Carlos, that went missing."

"So, what's going to happen?"

"Bobbie has friends around here. She went to find them to see what she can do. She will come up with something. Hopefully, this will be over tomorrow."

It all sounded doable. I just had to wait another day. If that were the case, another trip to never-never land would be nice. Why not? After everything that happened to me, I deserved it

"I don't know if I can make it 'til tomorrow. The pain is pretty bad. I winced and groaned. Closed my eyes like I couldn't stand the pain and reached down toward my broken leg so she'd get the picture. Can you get me just one more of those blue pills? Please."

"Is the pain that bad?"

"I won't tell Bobbie, I promise. Yeah, it's that bad."

She squeezed my hand and looked at me with sympathetic eyes.

I looked back, didn't blink, winced once.

"Okay," she said, and she left the room.

I tracked her footsteps to the duffel bag in the Captain's Room. I figured that's where the blue pills were stashed. A long silence ensued. Maybe they were packaged in such a way as to be difficult to remove. Then I heard Ashley's voice, "No, no."

She came back to the Author's Room.

"Cliff, I don't know whether you're telling me the truth or not—"

"Of course, I am. I have no reason to lie to you."

She smiled at that. "Yes, you do, and you wouldn't be the first one to do it."

Her bullshit detector was a little more advanced than I thought.

"Besides, I can't. Bobbie will kill me."

"Just one pill?"

"I can't. I told you. Please don't ask again." She raised both hands to signal me to back off. Her face was flushed red. She looked like she was going to explode. I couldn't tell whether it was going to be in anger or tears.

"Oh my god, Ashley. I won't if you don't want me to. I didn't mean to upset you." I meant it. I didn't want to give her any more angst. I pressed my lips with prayerful hands, and we just looked at each other. Sometimes, what is not said is more powerful than what is.

A door banged shut downstairs. Heavy footsteps pounded across the floor to the stairs.

"Ashley!"

"I'm upstairs." She wiped what remained of her tears.

"What the fuck are you doing up there?" Bobbie was not in a good mood.

"Nothing. Just bringing him some food."

"I need you down here."

Ashley whispered, "Gotta go."

BAD NEWS

Ashley ran down the stairs to greet Bobbie.

"What happened?"

"Nothing happened. That's the goddamn problem. None of my old friends seemed to know anything—the ones I could find anyway. They're all stuck in shitty eight-to-five jobs. No one has any money. I'm glad I left this place. There's nothing here for me. Nothing!"

"So what are we gonna do?" Ashley asked. Her voice quivered a bit.

"I know a few bars close by. I'll go out and find some buyers, see how much stuff I can move myself. It'll work."

"But I thought everything was closed up in the winter."

"Not the bars. They're open, and the gay bars are open past midnight. Filled too. You forget I used to live around here."

"That was years ago. Are the same people there?"

"Probably not. Maybe. I don't know. I'll meet new people. Jeez, Ashley, it would be a lot easier if you were with me instead of taking care of that jerk upstairs."

"Don't call him that. He's a good guy. Just in the wrong place at the wrong time."

"I can call him worse than that. He's like a canker sore. He's been plaguing me ever since he showed up."

"It's okay. Canker sores get better in a few days. Leave him to me. I will take care of him. You don't have to worry about it."

"Forget a canker. He's like a cancer. We have to find a way to—"

She whispered the next words. Maybe she said *cut it out.*

"And I don't want you talking to him." Her voice was louder, the words metered, more like a threat than a command.

"I have to talk to him to feed him and take him to the bathroom." Ashley sounded tentative and scared.

"I'm working my ass off. It's freezing cold out there. I haven't eaten. I haven't gone to the bathroom. And you're nursemaiding him!" Now she was shouting.

"I'm sorry, Bobbie." Ashley was crying through her words.

I heard Bobbie rip open the silverware drawer.

Ashley screamed, "What are you going to do?"

"I don't know what I'm going to do."

All I could picture was the big carving knife in that drawer and Bobbie with the devil in her eyes. If Missy was going to help me, now was a good time.

Ashley's voice rushed to Bobbie, "No, sit down. I made you some soup."

Things went quiet, like someone had hit the mute button right in the middle of a scene.

Finally, Ashley spoke in a soothing voice, "Go to the bathroom. I'll warm it up for you. Come on, honey. Everything's gonna work out all right."

I held my breath. *Come on, honey.*

Bobbie trotted off to the bathroom, and Ashley's footsteps hurried around the kitchen.

During Bobbie's late lunch, I stretched my ear to hear what they were saying, but their voices were softer than the clink of Bobbie's spoon on her soup bowl.

When it was over, Bobbie said, "I'm going up now."

Ashley said, "Okay."

Had Bobbie talked Ashley into getting rid of me? Had Ashley convinced her to let me go? I was one of those little animals caught in a trap, only I couldn't chew my foot off to get away.

Bobbie's heavy boots started up the back stairs.

Ashley's footsteps followed Bobbie's up the stairs—my heart started racing.

They got to the top of the stairs. Was Bobbie coming to cut out the cancer, or was Ashley coming to let the poor little animal go? I'd soon find out.

Neither happened. Bobbie went to the Captain's Room, where the drugs were stored, and stayed a while. Ashley gave me a ham and cheese sandwich with a soda and then went right downstairs again. Late afternoon was setting in when Bobbie headed back down without the duffel bag. She left right after.

The cold late afternoon air rushed up the back stairs when Bobbie left by the side kitchen door. As soon as she left, Ashley came upstairs.

"I thought I'd check if you had to go to the bathroom before Bobbie gets back."

"What's going to happen to me, Ashley?"

"Don't worry about it. It will only be a few more days."

"Yeah, but then what?"

"Do you need to go to the bathroom?"

"Yes, thank you." I didn't really have to go, but she didn't want to tell me what was happening, and I didn't want her to leave until I knew.

She unlocked me and helped me to my feet...foot. I put my arm over her shoulder.

"Are you okay, Ashley? It sounded pretty intense down there."

"It's okay. Bobbie just has a lot on her mind. She's not usually like that."

We started to buddy-hop to the tiny bathroom.

"I take it she didn't find a buyer for the . . . merchandise."

"No, but she's going to go out tonight to find one."

"Do you think she will?"

"Yeah, I think so. She knows all the bars. She used to live around here."

"Are the bars even open? It looks to me like everything around here is closed up tight."

"That's what I thought, too, but Bobbie said the gay bars are open to one o'clock in the morning, and they're real busy, even in the winter."

"I wouldn't know. I guess I never hung around gay bars."

"Me neither," she said. I took her to mean any kind of bar.

We passed by the Ocean Room and rounded the corner by the Captain's Room. I took note of the ladder built into the wall outside the Captain's room. I had forgotten about that. It looked like an 18-inch-wide built-in shelf with six thick, individual shelves. When the bottom was pulled out, the top slid down, and it became a ladder reaching the attic hatch above. For a moment, I thought that if I could get loose, I might find a way to sneak up into that attic and hide until they left, but then I realized that once I was up there, I had no way of sliding the ladder's mechanism back into its resting place in the wall.

"What if she can't find a buyer?"

"I'm worried about her now, but then I'll really be worried." She drew out the "really."

"Why is that?"

"Then she'll have to sell the . . . merchandise on the street, a little at a time."

"That would be awful." I was thinking of myself spending even one more day in that room, but Ashley had a different concern.

"Yeah, it could be dangerous."

"She seems pretty smart to me." It was as smart as a brick to keep the drugs in a duffel bag in the open like that, but I was trying to get into Ashley's frame of reference.

"Oh yeah, she is."

"Still, it sounds like you're on the horns of a dilemma."

"What do you mean?"

"Like there's no way out."

"No, I think Bobbie's gonna do it."

"I hope it works out for you. I'm sorry if I showed up and screwed everything up."

"It's not your fault that the deal she had fell through. That would have happened anyway."

"Then why are you worried?"

"If she sells too much in one place, she could step on some pretty mean toes, and if she doesn't sell big enough chunks, we won't get back to Florida in time to pay the people she borrowed money from."

"How much does she owe?"

She hesitated. I could see her thinking over the possibilities, but she wasn't going to tell me that much detail.

"A lot," she said.

At the bathroom, she left me alone to do whatever I was going to do and waited in the hallway. I asked through the door, "No, really. How much. Maybe I can help." It was an old trick I learned from years at the university. Someone who stays quiet during a faculty meeting drops their guard on a bathroom break.

"Fifty thousand dollars."

Had I gone to law school, I could have written out a check and been on my way, but a history professor doesn't have that kind of cash lying around. I was still paying off my lawyer and Penny's for the no-contest divorce.

"So, you're only fifty thousand dollars away from solving the problem?"

"Not exactly. The merchandise is worth one hundred thousand. The additional fifty thousand was supposed to give us a fresh start."

"I see the problem. That's too rich for my blood. I can't help you out."

"Thanks, I appreciate your asking."

When she tucked me back into bed, she didn't lock me up. The afternoon sun was disappearing behind the tree line, and she lit the candle on the bureau. She sat next to me on the bed. She had a far-off look in her eyes. "I wish—"

Just then, a set of headlights passed down the driveway to the back of the house.

"I gotta go." Ashley moved so fast that her fan flickered the candle.

BLISSFUL SPIRITS

The two of them were moving around the kitchen. Draws opened and closed.

Bobbie said, "It was Slim Pickens. Chatham bars were dead."

Ashley said, "Slim Pickens here too. We're running out of food."

I thought they were both too young to know who Slim Pickens was, but maybe it was a Kentucky thing. Bobbie said not to worry; she'd head out to Falmouth, where there was more action, and get something to eat at one of the clubs. She totally missed Ashley's problem that she didn't have enough food for herself or me.

They came upstairs together. Ashley gave me a bowl of tomato soup, some crackers, and water, then went right downstairs again. Bobbie went to the Captain's Room and stayed. Dusk was setting in when Bobbie headed back down. I got a glimpse of her carrying a gray gym pouch about half the size of the duffel bag that I had seen earlier in the Captain's Room. She left right afterward.

When Ashley came upstairs to clear the supper dishes, she lit an additional candle in a jar. It was nice to be out of the dark cellar and to have the moldy smell replaced by bayberry.

"Did you know this house was haunted?" I asked.

"What?" she said, and she turned around to face me.

"Do you believe in ghosts?" I asked.

"Of course, I believe in ghosts," she said. "I'm from Kentucky."

"Why is Kentucky a ghostly place?"

"We had all kinds of superstitions in Kentucky."

"Tell me about them."

She pulled the chair next to the bed. Seemed like I struck a chord with her—talk about Kentucky. Or maybe she was getting as stir-crazy and lonely as me.

"A lot of the superstitions came from the mountain people and the blacks—who had their hoodoo and charms. I lived in the lowlands, but we knew about ghosts and stuff."

"And what did you know?"

"Well, first, we knew every neighborhood had at least one haunted house. We kids used to go around trying to figure out which one it was."

"And how did you do that?"

"There were hints. If someone was murdered or met a horrible death in a house, that was a dead giveaway."

"A dead giveaway?" I drew out the word *dead.*

"Yeah, I mean, not just any dead. Dead by unnatural causes."

"Well, this house has a ghost." I emphasized the word "has."

"I kind of felt a little funny here, like there was a presence, especially in this room. How do you know there really is a ghost?"

"Well, I felt it too. But now I know. She lived on the land as a little girl, and when she got married, her husband built this house for her. He was a sea captain."

"How do you know all that?"

"I looked it up. I love history. Actually, I teach history in college."

"You're a history teacher?"

"I am. This house was built in 1850. Before that, the land was part of her father's farm. Of course, years before that, it belonged to the Indians—the Monomoyicks."

"Do their ghosts haunt the house too?"

"No, the Indians lived in huts on the land, and most of them died off or left because of the diseases that the Europeans brought when they landed here."

"In Kentucky, they said that if there was a dark moon on Halloween, the ghosts of departed Indians would ride the old trails."

"Well, when the ghost of this house got married, her widowed mother gave this parcel to her and her husband as a wedding gift, and they built this house. She lived here the rest of her life."

"And she still does?"

"I believe that the reason she's still here is because her husband, Captain Badishall, was lost at sea, and she is waiting for his return."

"See. I told you. An untimely death."

"That's not all. She had a young son who died of fever in this very room. In fact, the first time I saw her was in that closet."

"Right in that there closet?" She was smiling when she said it, not a mocking smile, a fun smile. "But that closet is locked."

"I know. I found the hidden key. When I opened the door and saw her, I got so frightened I jumped back and—"

I remembered something. When I jumped back, my head hit the pineapple on the top of the bedpost and broke it off.

"And what?"

"I conked my head on the bedpost."

"Did she attack you?"

"No, she just watched me make a fool of myself. I recovered my senses and asked her name. She told me it was Missy."

"She said, *Missy*? She actually talked to you?"

"Yes. Well, she didn't say it out loud. It was more like I could hear her voice in my head. But I distinctly heard the response, *Missy*. I found out later that her real name was Mercie, but I still call her Missy."

"And you really truly saw her."

"Well, I saw something, her form, I think it was, but it was plain as day. There one minute, gone the next." Ashley was right with me. Everything I saw and heard seemed perfectly believable to her, and she was enjoying the conversation.

"Did you know that horses can see ghosts?" she asked.

"No, I didn't."

"Yup. One time, my friend Gloria's horse was spooked by a ghost, and Gloria got right up over his ears—and she saw the ghost, too. She really did. Gloria was not one to tell fibs."

"Are you afraid of ghosts?" I asked.

"Depends. There are evil ghosts, and there are good ghosts. Sounds like Missy is a good one."

"I think so. She's probably listening to us right now."

"Hello, Missy." Ashley was very cordial and having fun with it.

"Missy, this is my friend Ashley."

Almost as if on cue, a rumble of thunder rolled over the house.

"Oh, oh! I don't think she likes you very much."

"I hope I didn't offend her."

"I'm just speculating here, but didn't you invade her house and hit her long-time friend Cliff over the head?"

"I think you're right. I better clear the dishes and get out of here."

She stood up, leaned forward, and placed her hand on my chest. For a moment, I thought she was going to kiss me on the forehead or cheek, but instead, she grabbed the napkin I had tucked into my shirt and then left with the tray of dishes and one of the burning candles.

When she finished cleaning up downstairs, the flicker of her candle rose on the back stairs. She approached the candle still burning next to my bed.

"Is there anything else you need before I turn in?"

I didn't want to face a long night of isolation. I had to think fast.

"You know, Ashley, there are a lot of mysteries in this world—things that happen that we don't understand or grasp the significance of."

"Oh, I couldn't agree more."

"Take this house for instance. This house is a mystery."

She put her candle on the nightstand next to mine.

"What do you mean?"

"It's a long story. Sit and I'll tell you, but you have to promise not to laugh at me or think I'm crazy."

"I won't laugh at you."

Good. She was still in a playful mood. She pulled up her chair.

"Before the summer that I first came to this house, my wife and I were in a car headed north into the Catskill Mountains of New York. The night air had become cold and foggy, and driving was tense. I could see the road in my headlights and hear the hum of tires speeding along on an asphalt. Our destination was South Fallsburg— a Siddha Yoga ashram."

"A what?"

"An ashram. It's a place where people go to meditate, pray, find wisdom. Our marriage was in trouble, and Baba Muktananda was the guru who supposedly had all the wisdom we were seeking."

"Is this about the house or about you and your wife?"

"Both, actually." Although, now, the story had become not only about the house and Penny but also about her. Ashley was pert, pretty, and blonde, with a turn-up nose. Penny had more of a classic Roman goddess look, dark hair, and straight features. One had just left my life, the other just entered, and the house was where we came together.

I continued my story. "We arrived at the ashram dog-tired. I needed sleep and didn't care that they separated men and women. My room reeked of burning incense. The other guys were already asleep in four bunk beds. The highway was still buzzing in my ears, and the hazy glow of a night light surrounded by burning incense reminded me of my headlights in the fog. I found an empty bunk, and five minutes later, I was fast asleep. The next part is pretty weird. You'll think I'm lying or I'm crazy."

"No, I won't think you're lying. Promise."

"I dreamed of a gypsy woman wearing a hood. She was holding the hand of a little boy. He looked just like me when I was a kid. The weird thing was—. Have you ever had a dream that was so real you felt like you were awake and actually living inside the dream?"

"I'm not sure."

"That's what it was like. I knew I was dreaming, but I was also there in the dream. I can describe every detail."

I was on a roll and had a captive audience. It was like telling a fairy tale at library hour.

"They walked on a cobblestone street, from one side of an arched entryway to the other. Halfway across, the gypsy woman stopped, looked straight at me, and scurried away. Her eyes told me she was taking the boy someplace where she could keep him safe. All I could think of was, *I have to tell Penny about this.*"

"Penny's your wife?"

"Yes. At breakfast, I recounted—in my usual great detail like I'm doing now—the room, the burning incense, the gypsy woman, and the little boy."

"I don't mind. What was your wife's reaction?"

"Her eyes kept scanning the room, the tables, the lines of people. She finally looked at me and said that I had hallucinated because of all that incense. Then she went to get in line for more granola and yogurt."

"She didn't believe you?"

"I think she believed me all right, but how can I say it? Penny had been falling out of love with me for a while, and at that point, breakfast was more appealing."

Ashley's face showed disappointment—maybe in Penny, maybe in love.

"But the weirdness didn't end there."

I used my spooky voice, and it got her attention.

"Later that morning, we were among hundreds sitting in a lotus position in a huge ballroom with Baba's disciple, Gurumayi Chidvilasananda—"

"That's a mouthful."

"Yes. She was sitting at the front, and we were so far back in the room that all I could make out was a saffron robe in the distance. It was the size of a half-munched carrot. Gurumayi said something that made everyone laugh. Then she laughed, and the room broke out in uncontrollable, infectious laughter. Penny laughed the way she used to. I did too. I closed my eyes and bathed in the joy."

Now Ashley smiled. She wanted me to be happy.

"After the meditation, Penny and I went to the ashram gift shop. I was looking for spiritual guidance in books by Eastern mystics. I'm a bookworm. I casually looked up, and my eyes were drawn to a picture on the wall."

I looked over Ashley's head, miming the experience.

"Shock hit me. I stepped back so hard into a bookshelf that it rocked back and forth. Penny helped steady the shelf. There on the wall was a large photo of the gypsy woman from my dream."

"Really?"

"Really! She was wearing the same hood, giving me the same look. I tell you, it was her! I asked the clerk who that woman was, and he said it was Gurumayi."

"There's that name again."

"Yup. During meditation, I couldn't see her face from a distance. But even if I had, it wouldn't matter. She came to me in my dream the night BEFORE I met her for the first time.

"That's amazing."

"Why did she enter my dream? Why was she taking the little boy inside me away for safekeeping? I believe there's a reason for everything."

"And what's the reason?"

"Penny and I were in couples counseling, and our marriage was facing the guillotine. Gurumayi was protecting my little boy from the pain to come. She was keeping him safe until I could find happiness again. I bought the photo and hung it in my study at home, but that's not the end of the story."

We had been talking for a long time. Ashley was getting fidgety.

"I'd love to hear the end of the story, but Bobbie may be home any time now."

"Okay, I'll make it quick. If we hear Bobbie coming, we'll just stop. You can run downstairs. We'll finish the story tomorrow."

That seemed to settle her down. I liked the fact that Ashley and I were planning strategies around Bobbie.

"Do you believe in fate, Ashley?"

"I guess."

"Well, I'll tell you the rest of the story, and you tell me whether you think it was coincidence or fate that brought me to this house."

I was about to tell her how fate brought me to the house to make up with Penny, but an idea was forming in my head that fate brought me back to the house to meet Ashley.

"It was shortly thereafter that we went to see the only summer house available in Chatham—this house. The view of the ocean outside the front bay window captured our attention. With the 1950s wood paneling that someone put up, that parlor is not a particularly spiritual setting. Right?"

She didn't answer right away. She was thinking. Then she said, "Oh my God! The picture. The picture in the bookcase. It's—"

"Right. You got it. Opposite the bay window was a floor-to-ceiling bookcase. I walked over to the bookcase and started scanning the books, left to right, top to bottom, looking for something interesting. All I found were Hardy Boys mysteries, James Patterson formulaic novels, and Jaqueline Suzanne drivel. A bunch of non-descript books with Yellow Umbrella bookmarks were likely purchased on the sidewalk in front of that bookstore for a dollar. The Bible and Koran sat together on a lonely shelf. You've seen them all?"

"And I've seen the picture."

"Yup. The last shelf on the right—someone made a little sacred place with a votive candle, an incense holder, a sage smudge stick—and that same photo of Gurumayi."

"The gypsy woman."

"The gypsy woman. Seeing that photo in that house sealed the deal. We rented it immediately. It had to be the hand of God directing us here. Gurumayi was his vehicle. It was fate."

"Sure seems that way."

"It didn't end there. I mean, she visited me in a dream. She protected my inner child. Made me rent this house. Then, after we got in here, she did one other thing."

"What?"

"Her photo kept slipping down in the photo frame. I'd fix it, and when we went back in, it would be cocked to one side or the other. Penny was spooked, and I figured Gurumaya was trying to tell us something strange was going on in the house."

"Oh my God! That was how we kids knew a house was haunted—pictures fell off the walls."

"That's why I started looking for Missy's ghost and why I found her. So, you tell me, was it fate or coincidence?

"Fate, for sure!"

"Think about it. She brought me here. Something brought you here. The little kid inside me is scared again, and in a lot of ways, you're taking care of him just like she did."

"But why is the ghost here?"

"I haven't figured that out yet. But I know this—my fate is now tied up with your fate. Why do you think we're both here together?"

Her mouth was open, but she didn't answer the question. A long moment went by.

"It's late, Cliff. Bobbie's due any minute. I have to go to bed. Do you need anything before I do?"

"No, I'm okay. Just think about it."

She set the bicycle lock and left me to face the night alone.

I wished I had a blue pill to help me sleep. I wished I had more time with Ashley. I could wish a hundred things, but I was here—and that wasn't going to change. How did I get here? A rhetorical question. I knew exactly how I got here: south on Route 3, cross the Sagamore, stick your nose where it doesn't belong.

How did I get here? was also a philosophical question. How did I get here at this point in my life? What little decisions and small turns made me into a divorced man with two kids, a shitty job, a headful of knowledge, and a bedful of nothing?

I was a late bloomer, mainly because I started school early. Mom enrolled me in first grade when I had just turned five. The boys in my class were always a foot taller; the girls always a bit smarter. I was lucky to utter a *duh* in any kind of social situation. By the time the girls sprouted breasts, I hadn't even popped my first pubic hair.

I figured out what Tommy Kelly and Gail Crosby were doing in the movie theater every Saturday, but I had as much chance of doing that as winning the Kentucky Derby.

I disappeared into my books. I became the hero of the Iliad and the Odyssey. I was the beast of Beowulf. I was Romeo. Sir Walter Scott. Even then, I hung out with ghosts. I was good at that. What I wasn't good at is I wasn't good at girls. Only in my dream world was I master and commander of my destiny.

Bobbie came home and interrupted my anxiety. It was probably way past midnight. She came upstairs and went into the Ocean Room, where Ashley was no doubt already asleep. They whispered a few minutes, but then everything went quiet. No squeaking bed springs.

Who cared?

All I wanted was to fall asleep, but I couldn't turn my chattering brain off. I had been a nerd in junior high, and I couldn't change that.

In the movie about the Nerds, the head cheerleader was impressed by the lovemaking of the head nerd, who explained his performance by saying that the only thing jocks think about is sports; nerds think about sex.

As I moved into high school, I counted on that, but I was still too small and too shy to make it happen—until one day in English Class. What a glorious day that was.

The assignment was to find a poem from the Romantic Period that I liked and give an oral report on it in class. For several days, one kid after another got up there and nervously reported on their love poems. It was a kind of Roses are Red, Violets are Blue festival, in which the poets were born, they suffered love, and they died.

Most of the boys swayed nervously from side to side, one hand in the pocket, racing to the final rhyme. Most of the girls got starry-eyed and swooned over their poems, placing a hand on their stomach or their heart. Roberta Tecci's presentation was memorable—not her poem, but her hand trying to find a respectable landing point not involving her ample chest.

I had long ago found a 19th-century poem by Algernon Charles Swinburne in a book of English love poems. In my fantasy world, I had already recited it to most of the girls in the class. Sophia Loren loved it, and so did Brigitte Bardot, even though I had never seen any of her movies.

I got up in front of the class. It was a warm spring day, and my love juices were flowing. I said, "Imagine you are on a picnic with your one true love. You're sitting under a shade tree on a hillside of green grasses and wildflowers." I stared off over the heads of my classmates and pointed. "All the way to the horizon is blue sky with tiny, powder puff clouds. You take out the poem you've written for the occasion."

I wasn't surprised to see them staring off into that blue sky. I was in the groove, and they were following. I read the first stanza:

> *If love were what the rose is,*
> *And I were like the leaf,*
> *Our lives would grow together*
> *In sad or singing weather,*
> *Blown fields or flowerful closes,*
> *Something, something, something*
> *If love were what the rose is,*
> *And I were like the leaf.*

You could have heard a rose or a leaf drop in the class.

> *If you were Queen of pleasure*
> *And I were King of pain*
> *We'd hunt down Love together,*
> *Pluck out his flying-feather,*

They were eating it up.

"Listen to the words," I told the class. "Pretend you didn't speak English—just the sound of the words carries the thought of love."

I finished the poem to dead silence, then applause. When a nerd turns into Casanova, there should be fanfare. Even the tough guys in the class came up to me at lunchtime to say I was a poet and didn't know it. What I didn't expect was that Joanne would wait for me after school.

"I wish someone would write me a poem like that," she said.

I walked her home. We made out in her front hallway. The next day, behind the gym, then at the drive-in. We went steady all through high school. I wrote her a hundred poems. Our parents met. We visited each other's grandmothers.

Then it happened.

The summer after graduation, she and her younger sister spent two weeks at her grandmother's cottage in northern Maine. I wrote her every day—upside-down stamp to declare my never-ending love. She wrote back: swimming in the lake, row boating, hamburgers and hot dogs—upside down stamp. The Saturday she got home, I hurried over to her house to show her the packet I had received in the mail from the college I was going to in September.

One section of the sidewalk on her street had collapsed. That didn't stop me. I sailed over it like Mercury with winged feet, while in my head, I was Robert Goulet singing that the pavement used to stay beneath my feet before. Her front door was ajar, and there at the bottom of the hallway stairs was her sister with her new boyfriend.

My momentum carried me past them. "Hi, glad to meet you." Is Joanne at—"

There at the top of the stairs was Joanne, with another kid. Not a kid. A man. I was a kid. She waved me through like a cop clearing a traffic jam.

"They're just leaving. Go inside. I'll be right with you."

My heart stopped beating.

When I showed her the pieces in my college packet, little pieces of my heart fell to the ground like cake crumbs.

How could she do that? I loved her so totally. Didn't she remember Algernon's poem? What about all the ones I wrote for her? Where could she find such a sensitive guy? Up in the goddamn woods of Maine! That's where. She was supposed to be visiting her grandmother, not finding a future husband.

Just because someone leaves you doesn't mean you stop loving them. All through freshman year, I acted as if she were my girlfriend away at another college. Half my heart had crumbled away, and yet I carried Joanne as my ghost-girlfriend in the half that was left.

Penny crushed that half when she agreed to the divorce.

What's wrong with women that they don't appreciate men as much as men appreciate them?

I tried rolling over slowly, but the wooden leg and bicycle chain limited my movement. Sweat accumulated on my back. I raised my body in an arch, and a loud squeak pierced the silence, followed by a second loud squeak and several soft ones when I landed. I stopped moving. Didn't want to wake my captors.

That was not entirely true. I wanted to wake Ashley.

"What's wrong? Are you okay, Cliff?"

"No. My body aches from lying so long on my back."

"Here, roll onto your side. I'll rub your back a bit."

With my luck, it would be Bobbie who came in, and she'd be carrying a baseball bat.

Hours went by. The ache in my body spread. My head started pounding, and my broken leg kept beating in synch. I wished I had a blue pill, a black pill, any damn pill at all. I just wanted sleep, relief from the private hell of my thoughts.

Missy, help me. Missy, help me. The more I repeated the words, the more I could feel her presence in the room—the one woman who had never left me. Her spirit could rest beside me. Soothe me. Calm me. The room grew lighter. My pains and agitation dissipated. If I listened hard, I would again hear her voice in my head.

"Sleep. Rest now. All will be well."

NEW DEALS

I woke to the sound of clinking dishes and the back door closing. I was using the lemonade pitcher when I heard a car crackle over the ice and stones in the driveway on the way out to the street. Soon after, Ashley came upstairs. She looked at me for a prolonged moment. She raised the shade on the driveway window slightly to get a better view in the morning light.

"Are you okay? You look awful."

"I am awful. I had an awful night." My night of hell must have shown on my face.

"The pain?"

"Ashley, I'm in agony. My leg hurts so much, and now my whole body aches from lying in this bed for 24 hours. You have to unlock my left leg. I have to move."

I could see her thinking about it, doing a calculation in her head.

"When's Bobbie coming back?" I asked.

"Okay," she said. She had the combination memorized and quickly freed my left leg from the bedpost leash.

I brought my knee up toward my chest and pulled on it.

"Bobbie?"

"She won't be back for a while, but when she does, I'll have to put the lock back on."

"I understand," I said. Ashley was beginning to trust me. She was less scared of what I might do than she was of what Bobbie might do. It was now Wednesday, and the drugs still hadn't been sold.

She said it would be good if I could sit up. I made a feeble attempt, but my beer-belly muscles wouldn't do the trick. She rolled me to one side, then the other, grasping me in a bear hug, and pulled me to an upright position.

"Your back is soaking wet," she said.

Then she propped the pillows up against the headboard and had me skootch backward. It was pretty simple to do, but I pretended the pain in my broken leg was too much for me.

"Sit up for a while. I'll go make you some breakfast."

I groaned, and she grimaced. She was feeling my pain. It was the perfect time to hit her up for another pill.

"Look," I said. "It's going to take Bobbie a few more days to sell the . . . merchandise. I'm in agony waiting."

"It may be longer than a few more days."

"Why?"

"Well, Bobbie went to Falmouth yesterday and came home with only $1250—not nearly enough. She's out now, but later today, she's heading to Hyannis. People there have more money."

"I didn't think she knew the Kennedys."

"Who?"

"Never mind. How about if you give me a couple of those blue pills to get me through the next couple of days?"

"You have to be careful. Those pills can be addictive."

"I'm not addicted. Even if I were, I can become un-addicted. What I can't do is make the pain go away. How about just a single pill?"

"I can't. It's too dangerous."

She said the words, but there was an uncertainty, a hesitation in her voice that I could exploit.

"Give me two good reasons why you can't."

"Bobbie will kill me."

An obvious exaggeration. Bobbie wasn't going to kill her. She wasn't even going to kill me. Bobbie was a bully, not a murderer. I just had to get through the next few days of pain—my leg, my body, my thoughts in the night.

"That's only one reason. One pill? Just to get me through tonight?"

"I can't. I can't. Please don't ask again." She wanted me to stop asking as much as I wanted her to get me a pill. In that moment, I wanted to take care of her.

"I won't if you don't want me to."

She laid her hand on my shoulder. "Stay sitting up. I'll get you breakfast."

By giving her what she wanted, I was getting something I wanted. I crooked my head onto her hand as if it were a soft pillow.

"Okay. Thank you for that."

A long second went by.

She slid her hand out and left the room.

Sometimes, what's not said is more powerful than what is said. Maybe I'd get a pill without the words, or maybe I'd just get more of her.

Ashley brought breakfast, coffee, toast, and a glass of water.

"I'm sorry. We're out of eggs and juice.

"It's okay. This is great."

"I also brought the Chatham History book that you mentioned last night. From the front parlor, where guru-whosie's picture is. Thought you might like to read it during the day."

"I appreciate that. Sit. Let's talk a minute."

She didn't say *What do you want to talk about?* She just pulled the chair over next to the bed and sat. I wasn't the only one alone with my thoughts marooned in a haunted house in Chatham.

"You told me about your father's death and your sisters holding back your inheritance, but you didn't tell me what went wrong between you and Bobbie."

"Nothing went wrong between us." She emphasized the word *between*. "It was just that Bobbie couldn't find good work, and there was some trouble at the hospital."

"Trouble? Tell me."

"There's not much to tell. I was the charge nurse working the night shift, you know, eleven to seven, at Memorial Hospital in the cancer ward."

"Wow. That's a lot of responsibility."

"Oh, I don't know."

I patted her knee. "It is, you know."

She wiggled uncomfortably in her chair, and I retracted my hand.

"Go on."

"Bobbie showed up around 6:00 AM with a croissant for me, and we shared a quick cup of coffee. We went into the room where the meds were stored for privacy. We were there for no more than ten minutes."

"And?"

"And that's all. I went back to work. When the day charge nurse came on the next morning, I turned over the key to the drug closet, and we discovered a lot of drugs—morphine and Oxy— had gone missing."

"How did that happen?"

"I don't know. All I know is suspicion fell on me, and when they did the investigation, it fell on Bobbie. It was awful. We had nothing to do with it."

She clasped her hands together like she was pleading for absolution.

"To this day, I don't know what happened to those drugs or who took them."

I untangled her clasped hands and held each one. I looked directly into her eyes—God, they were the bluest blue—now sparkling with rising tears, and I said, "I believe you."

And I did believe her. How could I not? Ashley wasn't made of the kind of stuff that would steal drugs or anything else. Bobbie would, but not that night.

I could see the gratitude in Ashley's eyes. I gently placed her hands between mine. "Tell me more."

She pulled her hands out of the warm cocoon I had created for her and threw them up in disbelief. "I was suspended pending a hearing. The police kept showing up at our apartment, harassing Bobbie and putting pressure on me to turn her in. There was nothing to turn in. Bobbie didn't take anything. We just ate our croissants and drank our coffee. Honest to God!"

"I believe you." This time, I rubbed her arms. "Do you think anyone else had a key?"

"I don't know. Maybe I had left it unlocked earlier in the evening when we did a round of meds. I've gone over it a hundred times in my head. I just don't know."

"You know what? Whoever did it saw Bobbie's visit as an opportunity to take the drugs and place the blame on her." My Columbo was working on her defense.

"Maybe. All I know is it was awful. Somehow, the local papers got the story. The headline said a nurse and her lover were suspected in the missing drugs. They named me and Bobbie in the article, even though the police never charged us with anything."

"Oh my god, I can't imagine what you went through."

"That wasn't the worst of it. My sisters found out and disowned me. Said I would never get my inheritance. Blamed Bobbie."

"What happened at the hearing?"

"We never got that far.

"All hell—heck—broke loose. Bobbie lost her job, and no one else would hire her."

Ashley grew silent. It looked like the whole sordid incident was replaying in her head. I was sorry to make her go through it again, but I still wanted to know more. I was searching for the words when she started talking again.

"I resigned before the hearing, and I let my nursing license expire. We couldn't pay our rent and got kicked out of our apartment."

A look of disbelief came over her face.

"We were out on the street. I just wanted to run away."

"I don't blame you. What did you do? How did you live?"

"We moved all the way across the state to Tampa, Ybor City, really. I got a job in an ice cream shop."

"And Bobbie?"

"Well, she was angry. She said if she was going to be accused of being a drug dealer, then she was going to get the benefit of being one."

"That's not exactly logical."

"I know, but what could I do? If it weren't for me, she wouldn't have been in that predicament."

I couldn't help but think that applied to me, too, but I kept silent and poker-faced.

"Turns out, Tampa is a center for the drug business, and it's crazy, but the bad publicity in Pompano Beach gave her a leg up getting started. Bobbie's pretty resourceful. It wasn't long before she worked her way up in the organization."

"How do you feel about it?"

"I don't like it, but what choice did we have? I lost my career, my family, my friends, my reputation, and Bobbie lost everything too—just because of me."

"You can't blame yourself—"

"I do. I should have been more careful. I trusted all my co-workers. Bobbie says I'm naïve, and I am. I trust people. You can't trust people anymore."

"It depends on who the people are." I let that sink in. "Ashley," I again took her hand, and she looked straight at me, "I want you to know something. You can trust me. You've had enough heartache to last a lifetime. I know what that feels like. I will never do anything to cause you more."

She used her sleeves to blot the tears from her eyes.

We heard Bobbie's car come up the driveway, and Ashley said, "I better go."

They spoke in hushed tones for a few minutes. It sounded like Ashley might have been pleading my case—reassuring Bobbie that I could be trusted not to turn them in. It could have gone either way. Ashley could be charming and persuasive, but Bobbie could be rash and unpredictable.

The next thing I knew, Bobbie's heavy footsteps were coming up the stairs. Adrenaline was pulsing through my body. I didn't know where she had gone all morning or what she intended to do with me. I couldn't plan my move without knowing her intention. I'd have to rely on instinct if she attacked me.

I took her in all at once. A glint from her eyes, her slow pace across the floor, no weapons in her hands.

"Hey, Bobbie." I choked out a greeting, trying to sound like I was running into an old friend at the library.

"Did you drive down here from wherever you came from?" Her tone seemed almost pleasant.

My vocal cords relaxed, and I answered, "From Boston."

"Then where's your car?"

"What?"

"Your car. Where's your car?"

"Why do you want to know that?"

"Never mind why." Her tone was edging toward belligerent. Then she dialed it back. "They may tow it away if we get a heavy snowfall. We should go get it, or you'll have no way of ever getting out of here."

Talk about prayers being answered.

"I parked it up near the Squire. "

"Where exactly?"

I pictured a football field and told her it was twenty-five yards past the Squire going toward the ocean, on the same side of the street. If I could have figured how many feet and inches, I would have told her that, too.

"It's a tan Toyota. The keys are in the coat I was wearing when—"

"I got the keys. I saw it was a Toyota. I just needed to know where it was so I could go get it."

"Thanks Bobbie. I think I can drive with one leg. If you get it for me, I'll be out of your hair. You'll never hear from me again. I promise."

I was hopeful for the for the first time in what? Three days? It didn't matter. All I wanted was to get out of there and get to the hospital. Get my leg set properly. Get home."

She headed for the door, then turned around.

"I don't want you putting any crazy ideas into Ashley's head. If you do, you'll be sorry."

"Ashley's taken good care of me. I appreciate that she has—that you let her. You don't have to worry about that. I just want to go home."

I pictured her and Ashley helping me down the skinny back stairs and into my idling car.

"You aren't going anywhere. I'm just getting your car. Then we'll figure out where you're going."

The cold afternoon air rushed up the back stairs when Bobbie left by the side kitchen door. If she were going out to her car, she'd leave by the back door. She was going to walk to the Squire to get my car.

As soon as she left, Ashley came upstairs.

"I thought I'd check if you had to go to the bathroom before Bobbie gets back."

"What's happening, Ashley?"

"I'm not sure. Bobbie went to get your car."

"Is she going to let me go?"

"Eventually, I think so, yes, just not right now. It'll only be a few more days. Don't worry about it."

"I do worry about it. I had no business barging in on you two, sticking my nose in where it doesn't belong. Now, I'm in a lot of trouble. Story of my life—not as dramatic as yours, but I sure could compete with you on troubles."

"You mean your divorce?"

"Yeah, but it goes way far before that. You don't want to know."

"Sure, I do. You listened to my story. I should listen to yours."

I don't know what possessed me, but I could feel myself falling for Ashley. Something inside me wanted her to know my story. "I don't know why it's up for me right now. I thought about it all night last night. Are you sure you want to know?"

"I'm sure."

"The girl I loved, the one who said we would someday marry, just up and ran off one day with someone else. For no reason. Well, she gave me a reason. She said that every year, when she spent time at her grandmother's summer place, she had a crush on this older boy, and when he finally noticed her, she couldn't say no.

I carried her around in my heart for years after that. Do you ever stop loving someone? I don't think that's possible. No matter what they do to you."

"I think you're right. I never stopped loving my father or my sisters for the way they treated me and Bobbie. What about your parents?"

"They're both gone now, too. I was close with my mother, but she kind of strangled me. She was not in favor of my going out with girls. When I met Joanne, my mother tried several times to break us up, and when we did break up, she had that I-told-you-so look on her face. I dated a lot of different girls in my college years, but none of them were good enough for her. To be honest, none of them were good enough for me. I was pining for Joanne."

"What about your father?"

"My father was a hard-working, stern man. When I changed my major in college from Accounting to History, he practically disowned me. How was I going to earn a living off of history? He never lived long enough to see me get a teaching job in college. My mother went into the hospital shortly after he died. That's where I met my wife."

"She was a nurse?"

"Yes. Much like you. Nurse of the Year in Nursing School."

"I was never Nurse of the Year."

"Yeah, but you said you were a very good nurse, and I say you're a very caring person. It shows. You can't hide it."

"Thank you, sir."

"You're welcomed, Madame."

We both had a chuckle.

"She was a very caring person at a time when I needed caring the most. We got married shortly after my mother died. I don't know; maybe we got married too quickly. We tried to get pregnant and couldn't. Then, we did and had a miscarriage. Then, when we had two kids, they were the world to us, but she and I were living in two different worlds. We both worked a lot and seldom spent time together. Vacations at this house in Chatham were the only real happy times we had together."

"Is that why you came down here, to remember those happy times.?"

"I don't know if I should tell you this, but I came down here to feel so bad that I would throw myself in the ocean—and end all this suffering."

I could see the empathy swell up in her eyes.

"Oh, Cliff, you musn't. You're a good person. There's someone out there who will love you for who you are."

"Thanks, Ashley. From talking to you, I'm beginning to believe anything is possible. Look, you know I'm not going to go to the police. How about you drop me off at the hospital? I'll get my leg fixed up properly—not that you didn't do a good job, but you don't have X-rays or anything to work with. As far as I'm concerned, you are Nurse of the Year."

I could see she was thinking about it, but I could also see the fear coming back in her face. She stood up.

"Let me think about it. I'll talk to Bobbie, and we'll try to work something out."

She gathered the breakfast dishes.

"I'll take these downstairs and be right back with your lunch."

Ashley didn't come right back with my lunch. Bobbie came home, and she still took priority. Evidently, Bobbie got my car and saw it was running on fumes. She said something about an idiot, and I assumed she meant me. The tank wasn't on super-empty. I had planned to fill up later that night. Then again, if I had jumped into the ocean, I wouldn't have needed gas where I was going.

I could hear them talking.

"Did you get gas?"

"Yes, and it was good luck that I did. I ran into Eddie Wheatley.

"Who?"

"Eddie Wheatley—we called him the weed in high school. His father was a doctor, and his mother a teacher, but Eddie was a pothead. We used to hang out together until he dropped out and had to go to work."

"Why is that good luck?"

"Well, in those days, he worked odd jobs, mostly on the docks, but the last few years, he's been working as crew on various fishing boats. He said he knows a captain who might be interested in buying what we have."

"When?"

"He didn't know for sure. The guy's not here all the time."

"Are you going to wait to hear?"

"No, I'll go to Hyannis. If I sell it there, then the fisherman will lose out. But I feel like our luck is changing. I think we're going to be all right."

"Sit down; I'll make you a sandwich."

Few words were spoken during their lunch, and those were mostly Ashley's whispers. I couldn't hear everything, but I got the sense she was pleading my case, slowly and deliberately, now that Bobbie was a little more relaxed about things.

"He's as desperate as we are."

I heard the word suicide.

"He's not going to go to the police."

The fact that Bobbie did not retort loudly gave me hope. Telling Ashley my sad story had its effect. It established some trust between us. The few civil words I spoke with Bobbie may have helped, too.

Maybe I wouldn't go to the police. Why should I? It would create a mess for me as well. I could just say I fell or something, and some good Samaritans put on a splint and dropped me off at the hospital.

Bobbie left for Hyannis—where the money was. She'd have little trouble selling the pills. They were pretty stupendous. I had never experienced such pleasure. Pharmacology was as good as sex. No, it was better. It was easier too. No dinner first, no jewelry, no endless hours of talking. One hundred percent reliable. No rejection.

One way or the other, Bobbie was going to sell the stuff, and I was going to go free. It was just a matter of time.

When Ashley came back upstairs, she was wearing her coat and boots. My heart jumped. She even handed me a cheese sandwich to feed me before we left.

She said, "I have to lock you up in case Bobbie comes back. I'm going to dash off to the market to pick up some milk and eggs. Is there anything you need before I go?"

What I needed, she wasn't going to give me.

For the first time in several days, I was alone in the house. It was an uneasy feeling, like that guy in the Dostoevsky book, alone on a high ledge staring into the darkness for an eternity, like I felt at night when Ashley and Bobbie were asleep.

If they were going to wait until tomorrow or the next day to free me, I needed to find some way to make it through the nights. I dreaded lying on my back for endless hours, unable to turn, alone with my feelings, my brain chattering like an aboriginal tribe in a frenzy.

If only she had left me unchained, I could have crawled my way to the stash and gotten my own blue pills. I looked down at the cuff around the bedpost and glanced up at the pineapple, which was too big to slip the cuff over.

Then I remembered when I first encountered Missy in the closet. I hit my head on the carved pineapple, and it broke off. I later repaired it by drilling a hole down into the bedpost and up into the pineapple. I inserted a two-sided wood screw and secured the pineapple back onto the bedpost. I did such a good job that it looked like it was all one integral unit. All I had to do was twist the pineapple off, and the handcuff could slide up and off—and this time, no beam was going to fall down to clobber me.

It was amazing how easily it came off. In less than a minute, I was free from the bedpost. Ashley was gone. I was alone in the house. I got up and hopped out of the bedroom, using the furniture for balance. Once in the corridor, I used the walls to steady myself all the way to the Captain's Room, where I found the duffel bag.

It contained two plastic bags full of hundreds of blue pills and one bag with small amber vials labeled LSD. There was enough space in the duffel to easily accommodate another three bags— likely the ones Bobbie took with her to Hyannis.

Bobbie would never miss even a handful of pills with the hundreds in the bags. I took three pills. I figured those would get me through the next few nights. Then I took two more for later, in case I wanted a little extra recreation. What the hell, I took another two for good measure.

I looked at the ladder built into the wall, but hiding them in the attic was too far away. I brought them back to the Author's room and wrapped them in a paper napkin left over from breakfast. I stuffed the package into the inside corner of one of my pillowcases and re-hooked the handcuff over the bedpost. Stuck the pineapple back on, and no one was the wiser.

I was proud of myself for outsmarting Bobbie. My stash was well hidden; hers was not. I could have done better than her with half my brain tied behind my back. It just takes a little ingenuity.

I could have stored them in the secret compartment under the bed. One time, my son dropped a bag of marbles on the floor, and I had to squeeze under the Author's bed to retrieve them. I noticed a knot hole in a two-foot-long board, and when I investigated, I found a nice little compartment under the wide pine board. Unfortunately, whatever treasure had been stored there in the old days had long been removed. I decided under the bed was overkill for my handful of pills. Besides, I wanted them close at hand.

I heard Ashley return up the driveway in my car and duck behind the house. She came in the back door and came upstairs.

"Are you okay? Do you need anything?"

Maybe she was concerned for my well-being; maybe she just wanted to make sure I was still there.

"I'm fine for now."

I was the picture of innocence, and I was fine—I was going to be even better later that night. "How did you like my car?"

"It was nice. Thank you."

She said it like I had let her use it out of the goodness of my heart.

"I've been thinking about what you asked me. If I drop you off at the hospital, how will you get your car back?"

I had to think fast.

"I figure I'll stay in the hospital a day or two. You two will be gone by then. Just leave the car in the back with the keys in it, and I'll take a taxi here to pick it up."

"What if we're not gone by then?"

I wasn't going to let this opportunity get away. I was on a roll anyway.

"If you're still here, it won't be a problem. Bobbie will know for sure that I'm trustworthy. She'll give me the car just to get rid of me."

"You have to promise me—promise me on a stack of Bibles—that you won't say anything to anybody."

"I told you. I wouldn't do anything that would give you one iota of consternation."

"Right now, I have to put away the groceries. I bought some good stuff for a healthy soup. I'll cook it up for supper tonight, and I have a surprise for you."

CHAPTER EIGHT
DREAMSCAPE

Night was setting in, and some delicious smells were rising from the kitchen. Ashley came upstairs carrying a pair of crutches.

"When I went out shopping, I poked around in the shed out back and found these crutches. Cleaned off the cobwebs for you." She propped them up next to the bed and lit the bayberry candle. "You won't have to lean on me when you go to the bathroom anymore."

Of course, I preferred to lean on her.

"You wanna try 'em?"

I looked at the bicycle lock.

She unlocked it.

I got up and hobbled around the bedroom on the crutches and my one good leg.

She said, "You're doing great. I also got you these."

She produced a small bag with one of those women's disposable razors and some shaving cream. "You take yourself to the bathroom, and I'll go down and get our supper."

Our supper. I liked the sound of that. I took the opportunity to spruce myself up a bit. Washed my face and wet down my hair, combing as best I could with my fingers. I even managed to shave several days of growth off my face and wash under my arms. I looked fairly presentable.

When I crutched back to the room, she had set up a coffee table with two bowls of steaming soup, a basket of fresh bread, some Parmesan cheese, and two sodas. Her hair was back in a ponytail and she had removed the apron she was wearing a short while ago. We made a good-looking couple.

"What's all this?" I asked.

"It's my specialty. A white bean soup with celery, carrots, onions, and spinach in chicken broth with diced tomatoes. Used to be my Daddy's favorite."

"Smells delicious. Has some exotic spices?"

"Salt and pepper. But maybe it's the Rosemary you're smelling or maybe the Herbes de Provence."

She pronounced *Herbes de Provence* the French way.

With the small table between us and the glow of the candle-light, we could have been in a restaurant in Paris.

"Have you ever been to France?" I asked

"France? Oh, gosh no. I've never been anywhere."

"You would love Paris." I would love to show her Paris. "Do you like art?"

"I guess." She handed me the Parmesan. "Sprinkle this over the top."

"Well, Paris is full of art. The *Musee du Louvre* has the most beautiful paintings and sculptures." I matched her *Herbes de Provence* with my *Musee du Louvre*. "You remind me of a painting I love there. It's a Rubin portrait of a peasant girl on a farm. I hope that doesn't offend you."

She didn't say anything. She just stared at the soup. I slurped a spoonful as softly as I could.

"No, I'm not offended. I'm a farm girl at heart."

"Yeah, I can see that. You have a wholesome look about you. Have you ever seen the Monet paintings of haystacks or ponds?" This was going well. I wanted to keep it going.

"I don't know. Are you okay sitting on the edge of the bed? How about if I prop up the pillows behind you?"

She got up and grabbed the pillows and wedged them up against my back.

I could smell the fragrance of her skin. It was a little like the soup, with a touch of sweat. The thought of her sweat intoxicated me. I gulped several spoons of soup. I wanted her to know I savored everything she gave me.

"Monet's paintings look like a thousand blobs of paint on a canvas, but when you step back, it turns into a beautiful scene."

"Oh yeah, I think I've seen one of those."

"Life is like that. Every moment of our lives is like a pastel blob on a canvas. We can't see its meaning until we get some distance, then it all becomes clear."

I could see her thinking about that. She had a slight smile on her face, as if I had just turned on a light for her. I decided to continue.

"Take us here right now. How we met. What's been happening the last couple of days? It's hard to discern what the big picture will become. What the future will hold. What would you like to see happen?"

She looked at me with those compassionate eyes and said, "Cliff, you know that I want you to—"

We heard a door bang shut downstairs. Her expression changed to one of fear. Heavy footsteps pounded across the floor to the stairs.

"Ashley!"

"I'm upstairs."

"What are you doing up there?"

"Nothing. Just bringing him some food."

"I need you down here."

"I'll be right down."

She hurriedly shushed me back into bed and locked my leash. Slid the card table with my soup dish next to the bed. She quickly lifted her chair and set it down like a cat's paws off to the side of the room, away from the bed and table. She ran her dish of soup into her bedroom, leaving no evidence of our eating together except for a brief splash on the floor.

She returned to squeeze my hand and said, "I've got to go," then sprinted out of the room.

If it could ever come to be, I'd take her to Paris. We'd have dinner in a little bistro, stroll hand-in-hand down the Champs-Élysées, and return to our little apartment in the Marais for a night of painted passion. I couldn't wait for my next blue pill.

Bobbie and Ashley had dinner together downstairs. Bobbie did all the talking. Ashley was quiet and never mentioned she was already having dinner with me in my room. She must have been sitting on pins and needles, worried that Bobbie would come upstairs for something.

Bobbie told her she had met some good people in Hyannis. They knew a place to crash in Provincetown and invited her to come along. They said they had a connection there who would buy all her stuff.

"I'll head down there tonight and meet up with them."

"Do you know them?"

"No, but they're good people. I can tell."

"Bobbie, you can't just go to P-Town with them."

"Stop worrying, Ashley. This is our way out. If it all goes well tonight, I'll bring the other half of the stuff down there tomorrow, and we'll be home free."

"What about Eddie?"

"I didn't hear back from him. If he comes through, maybe we can do another deal next year."

"I thought you told me this was it. We were going to make a new start in California."

"Yes, we will. I can't think about that now. I have too much else on my mind. Carlos disappeared. That jerk upstairs showed up. Leave me alone; I know what I'm doing."

Ashley didn't say anything. I could hear her cleaning up the dishes and pots and pans from the cooking she had done.

Bobbie went to the bathroom and returned, saying, "Don't wait up for me. I'll probably be very late." The wind whistled in through the back door when she left, and Ashley remained quiet in the kitchen for quite a while. She came up and retrieved my soup dish, utensils, and the bread basket.

"Are you okay, Ash?"

I could tell she looked over at me, but in the dim light, it was too dark to see her expression.

"I'm okay," she said, but it was an *okay* that meant *I'm not okay, but there's nothing I can do about it.* She went into the Ocean Room to retrieve her dish of cold soup and carried it downstairs. When she finished cleaning up all the dishes and pans, she came back upstairs carrying a single candle.

"Cliff, it's been a long day. I want to turn in." She walked toward me. The candlelight danced across her pretty cheeks and kissed her perfect lips—the reflection returned to me in her eyes. Then she touched my leg. "You have everything you need?"

In that moment, I did.

The light from her candle floated out of the Author's Room toward the Ocean Room and finally disappeared. I was alone again.

I reached into my pillowcase for a blue pill.

The pleasure began to take over my body like a radioactive dye being mainlined into my carotid artery. A crimson-red heat flowed down my neck and filled my shoulders. Why crimson red? Who cares? It felt Tony-the-tiger grrrrrreat.

I wanted more. I willed the pleasure to fill my body, and my spine began to vibrate, radiating crimson pleasure outward across my upper torso. Not only did I wallow in the pleasure, but I became intoxicated with the power my will afforded me. Reality became slave to my will.

I bade Ashley to lie beside me, her petite body next to mine. The heat of her breath tiptoed across my neck. Her soft breasts were so tightly pressed against my chest that our hearts seemed to beat as one.

The crimson engulfed our entwined bodies. I pressed for more. And more.

Challenge the cosmos.

The last rush came like a thunderclap, a lightning burst, and a sky jump into the night. Then nothing. I slept like a jellyfish floating in a sea of darkness.

Time may have stopped. It may have accelerated. I don't know. I wasn't in a world where time mattered—until I felt myself moving downward in the dark. I braced for a landing, but I just kept dropping, not like a roller coaster, more like a descending elevator.

As I passed each floor, I got a glimpse of the scene: my mother and father shaking their heads in disapproval, Joanne laughing with her husband, Penny and the kids sitting around the table with my empty chair.

Fear seized me. I saw Bobbie's face through the oblong window of the front door. The falling accelerated. I barely perceived Ashley wielding the skillet before the elevator crashed at the bottom, and I again felt the pain of the beam breaking my leg.

I lay on my back in the quiet aftermath. My eyes adjusted to the shadows—sloping walls, a skinny door, two bedposts. I had landed in the back-stairs bedroom at the top of the skinny, little stairs. The words kept reverberating in my head. *The bedroom at the top of the skinny, little stairs.*

I became hyper-aware of the squeaky mattress and my leg chained at the foot of the bed. There, between the bedpost and the closet door, was the dark silhouette of a woman.

"Ashley, is that you?"

No answer came.

"Gurumayi?"

"No, silly. It's me."

She stepped into the light, or to be more precise, she became the light. Her brown hair was neatly tucked into a white lace bonnet. A white apron protected her head-to-toe, blue dress that seemed to be made of puffy layers of plain cloth.

"Who . . . who are you?"

"Why, I'm Mercie Badishall, Everett's wife, although he's been gone many a year."

Was I still under the influence of the blue pill? Was I dreaming?

"Are you really here?"

She and I were both speaking in hushed tones rather than through ghost-talk, but somehow, the fact that we were having an actual conversation didn't seem strange to me. Maybe it was the blue pill. Maybe she had been there at the foot of the bed all the time, just not—what's the right word—manifested?

"Of course, I'm here. This is my son's bedroom; may God rest his precious little soul."

"I didn't expect—"

"This is my home. You knew that, calling me Missy and all. You're a sweet butter, you are."

"But why are you here?"

"That's a good question. I've asked myself that many times, but truth be told, I've always been here."

"Always?"

"Well, ever since I was a little girl. This was my Pa's farmland, and my sisters and I used to come here and play long before the house was here. In those days, there was still an abandoned Indian hut out back, and we used it as a playhouse."

"The Monomoyicks?"

"Monomoyick Village. They belonged to the Wampanoag. They were here long before the settlers. No teepees for them. The huts were more sturdy—round, wood and reeds and bark, warm in the winter and cool in the summer. They were all gone by time I was born, but I was born on this land—played on it as a little girl, lived on it as a married woman."

"You went from the hut to the house." I was being clever, and I wanted her to know I was listening.

"Yes, Everett built the house, he and the neighbors, and the people he hired. Took a whole year to build."

"And you and he lived here your whole lives."

"Well, yes and no. My son died of the fever when he was just five years old." She said it matter-of-factly, like the old wound had long ago healed. Then she got pensive, "Hadn't even got into school yet." Now, she seemed to have a hint of lament. "The good lord took him too soon."

If she said another word, tears would have come. Time hadn't healed the wound after all. The loss of her child had been such an emotional overload that she locked up her grief like she locked up that closet.

She was letting me have a peek inside. Of course, I already knew the facts. I had researched her and her family. I didn't know what to say. Life was so hard in those days. People died at young ages of the fever, the palsy, childbirth, or a myriad of mysterious causes.

The other great loss in her life was her husband. Now that the door to her grief was opened, I was listening for that. She went on.

"Then there was that terrible day in November—"

"When Everett—"

"Yes. The Fall fishing season was drawing to a close. He went out on his schooner, the Resurrection. He wanted to make one last catch before winter set in. He had the deck filled with dories and an able crew to launch them."

She seemed to trail off into thought, and I finally broke the silence.

"What happened?"

"Well, I went out in the morning to feed the chickens and gather eggs. The air had turned extra cold. Rain barrels had a thin coating of ice on top. The sky became dark, and strong onshore winds were gusting. Sails can handle steady winds. It's the gusty winds that give ships their trouble. When I looked out at the ocean, I could see black storm clouds with lightning strikes on the horizon. Whatever was heading my way had already wreaked its havoc at sea."

She was looking off into space toward the sea. You can tell when people's minds wander off to another time and place. It's even more obvious when a ghost does. She needed a little nudge to go on. "What came your way?" I asked.

"Snow. A Portland gale. A wrath-of-God storm."

"Do you know what happened to him?"

"It was the next day. The men from the Lifesaving Service—they used to patrol the beaches during storms—came to my house. One of the Dories had washed ashore with a crew member near frozen to death. He said the storm came up all of a sudden like. The dories were off the ship with their trawl lines out, and Everett was ringing the ship's bell, calling them back in. Then, the Resurrection took a lightning hit. The main mast came crashing down at the same time that a giant wave hit. The schooner rolled over and went down fast."

She said it the same way she said her son died of fever—with little emotion. It's the same for people and ghosts. When emotions are too painful to recall, some protection mechanism kicks in, and your memory of the happening converts into little more than a travel itinerary. The mast came down. The schooner rolled. It went down fast. All I said was, "That's a tragic story."

"Too common a story. Many a good Chatham man was shipwrecked. Some survived. Some came back shadows of themselves."

She paused for a long time.

"I never saw Everett again."

"Did you ever hope that he would return?"

"Hope? Hope is eternal. I have often stared out at the night during an ocean storm and pictured Everett at the helm of the Resurrection—the sails filled with wind. I have imagined the ship emerging from the storm, its hull riding high on a wave and crashing down on a course set for home. Hope is really a prayer. It's a widow's duty to hope, to pray."

Her words seemed wistful like it was one more daily chore to which she was resigned—feed the chickens, cook the food, and pray. Then she leaned forward with her hands grasping the bed. "And it's a widow's duty to wait."

What a woman. She waited over one hundred years for her husband to return. I was impressed.

"Did you ever think of remarrying?"

"Many a widow remarry, but usually because they need a man to provide. I had the means. Besides, no man ever came along and paid me much attention." Then she paused again. This time, a short pause. She seemed almost embarrassed, a little coquettish.

"Until you came along."

"Me?"

"I've watched people come and go in this house. Some treat it with respect, some not so much. I watched you and your family for many years. You were always respectful."

"Thank you. I try to be."

"I was surprised when you called me out."

"Somehow, I always knew you were here."

"And then you did so much work finding out about me. I was flattered. Every summer when you returned, it was as if I were being courted again."

"I wish I could have courted a woman like you. Someone who would wait a hundred years for my return. You're the kind of woman I always prayed for."

"It does my heart good to know a man who appreciates a good woman. You're a good man. But then I knew that when I watched you in contemplation of the Bible."

She must have seen me perusing the Bible in the front parlor. I like the history recorded in it, especially as it relates to the origin of today's problems in the Mid-East. I've even read those Gideon Bibles we used to find in hotels and motels. The doctrine varies in different versions of the Bible, but the historical events remain pretty consistent.

"Yes," I said, "but the reason I read the Bible is—"

"No matter. You spend time with your Bible. That's all that counts, and you have a proper reverence for my home. These other two creatures have defiled it. They brought evil into these walls. It's sinful!"

"They are sinners." I was channeling my Baptist preacher.

"I'll help you rid yourself of them, but you must be free from sin."

"What do you mean?"

"I understand that you are a man, and men sometimes have lascivious ways."

"Lascivious ways?"

"I can see the way you lust after that girl."

"That girl?"

"The one named after the ashes of hell."

"No, no, you misinterpret my intentions. I feel sorry for her."

All I could think of was the Shakespeare line about she doth protest too much. But if Missy was going to help me, I had to be the one in the house who was free from sin, and I was. I hadn't done any of the things I dreamt of doing with Ashley, and ever since Jimmy Carter, impure thoughts have been reclassified as Presidential. Still, I wanted to come to Ashley's defense.

"Ashley's under the influence of the other one, and it is the other one that has gotten her caught up in the sin of lascivious ways."

"Lascivious ways? No, there have been no sins of lascivious ways in my house." She emphasized the word *my.* "They have brought no men here. Their great sin is making a prisoner of you."

"Even though they're two women sleeping together?" I figured back in 1850-Chatham, that was considered lascivious. I reiterated, "Sleeping together. Two women sleeping together."

"I slept with my sisters all through the cold winter nights." She said.

"I don't mean like that. I mean, they are sleep-ing together."

"Yes. You said that."

"I mean, in the same way you and your husband slept together."

Still, Missy seemed puzzled.

"I mean—how should I say this—did you and Everett ever do anything . . . more than have intercourse."

"Why, of course we did. I cooked and cleaned. Kept the chickens and rabbits fed. Tended the garden. Everett had all he could do to operate the schooner, sell the fish, keep the crews happy."

I didn't know how else to put it. "They're sleeping together in the biblical sense. They're having sex."

Her eyes and her mouth opened wide. "Are they harlots?" She covered her mouth as if she should not have asked the question.

The conversation was going off track. I didn't care about Bobbie and Ashley's sex life. Well, not that much, anyway. I wanted to focus on how Missy might help me get away.

"Missy!"

She looked at me, but still on her face was a look of disbelief—or was it disgust?

"You've got to help me. What can we do to set me free?"

She raised her eyes to heaven to receive her answer. "Samuel Chapter 26 Verse 8?"

All well and good, that didn't help me. "I'm not sure I remember that passage."

"God hath delivered thine enemies into thine hand this day: now therefore you shall smite them."

"I will? How?"

She reached into the pocket of her apron and pulled out a pair of long, pointed shears, which she raised to eye level.

"By God's own messenger."

"Who's that?"

"I am God's messenger, and those harlots are thine enemies."

"Not Ashley? I think she's under the influence of the other harlot, I mean the other one, Bobbie. I think Bobbie is mine enemy." Why was I talking Bible?

"Besides, I'm thinking Ashley might set me free. She might even convince Bobbie to let me go."

"Beware! False prophets fill you with false hopes—Jeremiah 23:16."

I didn't want to argue with her about scripture or who was and who was not a harlot.

"All I want to do is get out of there. Can you help me do that?"

She repeated, "We shall smite thine enemies."

I didn't really want to smite anyone. I have never wanted to smite anyone. Well, that wasn't exactly true. The bastard that took Joanne away from me ruined my life. I wouldn't mind seeing him struck down. I'm not really a smiting kind of guy, but some people just plain deserve to be whatever the past tense of smite is.

Maybe my old boss, Mr. Morrison, too. Gave my job to his son, after all I did to help his business. If he wasn't dead already, I could deep-six him.

Some people could do with a good flogging or a public shaming. Professor Dolan for giving me that D in American History. Why did I have to show up to class when I aced all the exams? He should be exposed. He's not a teacher; he's an enforcer.

How about the parents of that little bastard on the minibike who lived next door to Penny and me in Winchester? Around and around he went with that incessant noise. I couldn't hear myself think. Add him and his mother to the pile of reprobates.

Throw in Charlie Pestucci for de-pantsing me in sixth grade and the idiot judge who—.

"You do go on." Missy seemed to be chiding me as if, in the long silence, she read my thoughts. I hoped she couldn't read my thoughts.

Just then, a small candlelight flame floated into the room. As it drew closer, Missy's shadow retreated, and then she was gone.

"Who are you talking to?"

It was Ashley's voice.

"Do you need something?" She sounded like she was whispering inside an echo chamber. I stirred. I might have said *no*, or *I am sleeping, or I am dreaming.* All those thoughts went through my head, but I didn't voice them—the effects of the blue pill were still with me. Ashley's sweet voice again brought the crimson pleasure flowing in my body.

The candlelight grew brighter. The flame was so close to my face that I could feel its heat. It was as if I were on a beach looking up at the sun. At first, I thought it was a tropical beach in some future life when my leg was healed, and Ashley was done with Bobbie. But then the light dimmed. I had the sense that Ashley left the room, but I wasn't in the room. I was on the little beach at the end of Holway Street, where I lost those happy summers with Penny and the kids.

I was alone. Alone again. Always alone.

I had no sense of where I was going. In my hands was a map that Samuel de Champlain had given me. On the horizon, the French fleurs-de-lis flying on the topmast of his sailing ship dipped lower and lower into the horizon. Then, it was gone.

I had missed the tide that launched the ship on its journey back to Europe. Maybe the ship was filled with fresh cod harvested from these waters, salted and stacked chest high in the hold below. Maybe they had traded with the savages that greeted them on shore, giving them treasures from the civilized world in exchange for their blankets, furs, and especially their land.

Only the caw of an occasional seabird broke the soft sounds of the wind and the ocean.

With the tide low, the air still held some summer warmth, but the soft onshore breeze carried a chill. Soon, summer would be gone. Winter was inevitable. A gull dove into the dark waters.

I walked up the dunes toward the small Indian village on the map. Sandpits filled with Indian corn were exposed. No one was tending the food stores for the winter. At the top of the hill, where the house was supposed to be, a cluster of huts sat surrounded by this year's corn crops, withering on the vine.

One hut's chimney had smoke. I walked over. An Indian of considerable height lay helpless inside. From the size of his shoulders and thighs, he must have once been a fierce warrior. Now, his emaciated body struggled for breath. Next to him was a telescope made by a skilled optician in London and transported in the hold of the ship that had just sailed. In his blood was a virus/bacterium tailor-made for him in the rat-infested gutters of London and carried in the hold of that ship.

When the Indians were many, and the settlers were few, land was plentiful. The Indians freely gave lands to the settlers without understanding that the gifts they received in exchange and the papers they laid their marks on would forever make that land the property of these strangers. By the time the settlers were many, and disease had made the Indians few, it was too late to do anything but move away from the white settlements.

This Indian had decided not to move—he was going to die near the ocean he fished, next to the corn field his wife tended, in the hut he built for his family.

He looked up at me and spoke in a tongue I didn't recognize, but his eyes said, *Leave me to die in peace.* I had no business being there, so I left repulsed by the remnants of the bloodless conquest that we made of these indigenous people.

The old history recorded that the noble settlers brought civilization to the savage Indians, but the new history says the savage settlers brought death and destruction to the noble Indians.

I watched my feet walk upon the land. It was just dirt beneath my feet. No gold, no riches. Why did a whole race have to be annihilated to secure it?

When I looked up, I saw the house in all its majestic beauty. I turned back, and the village and the crops were gone. Only the one hut I had been in remained. Three young girls were giggling and playing outside. I glanced back at the house, and it was gone. The giggling ceased, and the girls and the hut were gone.

I was again alone with no fixed time in which to live, no place to call home, haunted by ghosts of the past. None of that mattered. I needed sleep. I needed the freight train that was my body to uncouple from the engine that was my brain. I pulled the connecting pin and lay immobile as my consciousness chugged off into the horizon.

The bed sunk, and the bedsprings squeaked. There was a time when the woman sleeping next to me would roll over, and the bed would move. You get used to those motions in the night and stop noticing them. You never get used to your bed having no one to disturb it.

"Cliff, are you awake?"

It was Ashley's voice. This time, no echo chamber. If anything, her voice quivered in her throat, anxious, despairing even. It didn't matter to me. Ashley was back. I braced for the crimson waves of ecstasy to break over me. They didn't come. My body was craving sleep, not excitement.

A hand touched my shoulder. Gave a little shake. Ashley—in the flesh. She whispered in the dawn light, "Cliff, it's me, Ashley."

"Ash, what happened?"

"Nothing. Nothing happened. Bobbie never came home."

"Didn't she go to P-Town?"

"Yes, but she should have been home by now."

"Do you think something happened to her?"

The question took her aback. Her countenance changed from worry to shock.

"No, I don't think that. Bobbie's too smart for that. Too careful. Too—I don't know—that's not what I'm worried about."

"Then what?"

She sat side-saddle on the bed next to me. "I'm worried that she's gone back to her old ways. I was afraid of that when she said she wanted to come back to the Cape."

I propped myself up on one elbow. "What are her old ways?"

Ashley started crying. "You know. She slept around. But that was a long time ago. She was a different person then."

"Different how?"

"She was lost—like I was lost." The word *lost* was said as if its sound were the same as its meaning.

She seemed suspended in her memories. God knows she suffered plenty of losses—her father, sisters, job, and now maybe Bobbie, too. She looked at me with empty eyes. "I don't know what to do!"

With that, a flood of emotion erupted—tears, sobbing, her head and hands thrashing.

I touched her shoulder, and she melted down into the comforter on my chest.

I scooched over and put my arm around her. "It's okay, Ashley. Cry it out. It's okay." I coaxed her into crying on half of my pillow. She twisted to lay next to me, and I said, "Wait. You'll freeze."

I raised the comforter, and she glided in next to me, her body warming mine. She continued to sob, now into my shoulder rather than the pillow. I reveled in it. Her tears blessed me like holy water.

I let her cry until the sobs subsided.

"Talk to me. Tell me how you feel inside."

"Bobbie met a woman in Hyannis who had a place to stay in P-Town. Bobbie went down there with her, and she said this girl could hook her up with someone who would buy a large quantity."

"Don't you believe her?"

"I don't know what to believe. She didn't come home. She didn't call. She's with that woman. I know it. I could tell, just by the way she talked about her. Like she was exciting, worldly—all the things I'm not."

"You're more than that. You're sweet, you're caring, you're beautiful. Anyone would be blessed to have your love."

"You don't understand. All that trouble with my job at the hospital—it was like a drug to Bobbie. She loved the challenge. Something to overcome. Something with a monkey wrench in it that she could come in and fix. I didn't want her to get into drugs. She convinced me it was the only way out. The only way we could get a new start. But when it worked last year, she was ecstatic. She wanted more. She liked the danger. The intrigue. It was like the life she gave up when she met me. She missed it."

"That life's not for you."

"I know. I gave Bobbie an ultimatum. Give it up, or I'll leave. She said just one more time. She said it would set us up, then we could go to California and start over at a normal life. She promised."

"Well, maybe she still means it."

"Then why didn't she call? She was supposed to come home last night."

By now, the Thursday sun had come up. Ashley and I were wrapped in the comforter. Her arm was looped across my chest, and we were talking like husband and wife, her head resting on my shoulder and my cheek against her hair. Every once in a while, she'd raise her head to say something she wanted to emphasize, but then she'd return to our snuggled position. I wanted to reassure her. I thought little about myself or how good it felt to have such a warm woman clinging to my side.

"Look, Ashley, I don't want to worry you, but there is another explanation that means she didn't betray you."

"What do you mean?"

"I'm reluctant to say, but you have to consider it a possibility. She's dealing with some shady people. Something bad could have happened to her."

She swiveled back to sitting up on the side of the bed. The cold morning air chilled all the places on my body where hers had been.

"That would be better. No!" she shouted. "What's wrong with me? I don't want anything bad to happen to Bobbie. Oh my god. I don't know what I want. I'd rather she was shacked up with that woman than beat up or dead on the side of the road."

"Have you tried calling her?"

"I called her before I came in here. I got *the person you called is unavailable right now.* I sent a text. No reply. Do you think she's hurt?"

"Maybe her phone's off, or she's in an area with no service."

I tried to sit up, but the shackled leg prevented me from moving next to her.

"Unlock that stupid thing. We'll figure something out."

She undid the lock, and I sat on the side of the bed. She was now standing.

"Come here." I guided her down beside me and put my arm around her. "Whatever it is, we'll figure out what to do next." She just sat there staring at the floor. I hadn't noticed before, but she was clutching her cell phone the whole time. "If something has happened to her, would the police call you?"

"I don't know. I'm in her cell phone, but I'm not sure how I'm listed. There are lots of names and numbers in there."

"Do you want to call the police in P-Town and see if they have any information?"

"No!" She was vehement. "We can do that. If she's with that woman, and if they're selling the drugs, she'll be in so much trouble. No police. That's Bobbie's rule. Always."

"Well, how about if you and I jump in my car and head down there? You can keep calling, and we can look around P-Town for her car. It's not that big of a place."

"But what if she comes back here and we're gone? She'll kill me."

"Then, we'll just have to wait. Things will become clearer as the day goes on. Right now," I reached for my crutches, "I have to pee."

"Me too," she said.

"Shall we go together or take turns?"

A laugh burst out of her and ended in an almost cry. She smiled at me. It was the kind of smile that said I'm glad you're here. She stood up again.

"You go pee in the telephone booth bathroom, and I'll go pee downstairs. I'll make us some coffee."

We sat side by side in the bed, drinking our coffee. She remembered how I liked it—milk, no sugar. She made some toast. I said, "You get crumbs in this bed, I'm moving into your room."

She laughed again.

I added, "And when Bobbie comes back, she'll be sleeping with me. Then you'll be sorry."

"Oh, Cliff, I don't know anything anymore."

She put her coffee mug down on the nightstand and moved the dish of toast there, too. She looked at me in a way she hadn't before. I handed her my coffee cup and held her gaze. She turned away to lay it down next to hers. She turned back, and, as if it were the most natural thing in the world, a strand of her hair lay against my face, her scent wafted into my brain, and the taste of her lips lingered on mine. I was back in the ecstasy of the crimson wave.

PLAN C

Where was I? I don't know. Somewhere between Nirvana and the Sagamore Bridge. The first restful sleep I had had in months. No wine. No Melatonin. No antihistamines. The blue pill had worn off. The warmth of Ashley's body sculpted against mine conjured up the two of us lying in an embrace on a deserted Caribbean beach. The future was calling me like the trailer of an exciting new film.

When a car came up the driveway, Ashley jumped up.

"Oh my god. Bobbie's home."

I tried holding on to her, but she spun around like a dervish and my warm body was chilled with cold air. She darted into the other room in her T-shirt. Those bare legs had kept me so warm for so many hours.

Thirty seconds later, she flew by my room wearing her sweats. By the time Bobbie opened the back door, Ashley was downstairs waiting.

"Where have you been?" Her tone was demanding. It carried a bunch of unsaid words—*Where the hell have you been? What do you think you're doing? I want no part of this!*

"I was robbed." Bobbie's tone was apologetic. *I'm sorry* was painted all over it.

"What do you mean I was robbed? By who?"

"I don't know. We slept in a vacant art studio, and when I woke up this morning—"

"Who's we?"

"Veronika and her friend. I told you. The women I met in Hyannis. They were going to hook me up with—"

"You didn't tell me you were going to sleep with her."

"I didn't sleep WITH her. We all slept in an art studio they knew would be empty. They were going to take me to the place in the morning."

"What place?"

Something had ignited inside of Ashley. She was no longer the timid Kentucky girl being taken care of. She had turned into Atticus Finch in court. Bobbie was stuttering and stalling like a guilty defendant.

"The place where I was going to sell the drugs."

"And why didn't you?"

"I was trying to explain it to you. When I woke up in the morning, the drugs were gone."

"What do you mean they were gone."

"Gone. Like they weren't there anymore."

"Fifty thousand dollars' worth? Gone? Just like that? Where were they?"

"They were locked in the car. Hidden in the spare-tire compartment. Under the boot."

"Did you meet the guy who was going to buy the drugs?"

"I told you, they were gone."

"I heard you. But did you meet the guy?"

"What does that matter?"

"The other half. You have the other half upstairs. Another fifty thousand dollars' worth. If he buys that, you could at least get out of debt with the people in Florida."

"No, I didn't meet him. They were gone when I got up."

"Who was gone?"

"The two women."

"Veronika and her friend?" The words were dripping with sarcasm.

"Yes. I told you. When I woke up in the morning, they were gone."

"The women were gone, or the drugs were gone?"

"Both. Look, Ashley, I'm sorry. I screwed up royally."

"Did they break into our car?"

"No. They must have taken the keys out of my pants while I was sleeping."

"You slept with them—correction, not WITH them—just without your pants?"

"How did they know where the drugs were?"

"I don't know. Maybe I said something."

"Were you drinking?"

"I had a few drinks, but—"

"You're lucky they didn't steal the car—or your pants!"

Ashley came storming up the stairs. She passed by my room and went into the Ocean Room, slamming the door behind her.

The two of them remained quiet for several hours, Ashley upstairs, Bobbie down. Just after noon, Bobbie went into the kitchen and was busy doing something. Shortly after, she came quietly up the back stairs carrying a tray full of food. She gave me a sandwich, a soda, and a piece of store-bought pie. She seemed quite contrite.

I said, "Thanks. Hey Bobbie, I heard what happened—"

"Shut up!"

She pointed a finger at me and had the same fire in her eyes she had the first night I caused trouble—a poster child for *if looks could kill*. Evidently, her contrition wasn't for my benefit.

She didn't stay long enough to notice I was still unlocked from my leash. She took the tray with more food on it and knocked on Ashley's closed door.

"Can I come in? I made you some lunch."

Ashley didn't answer.

Bobbie entered the room and said, "Look, Ashley, I screwed up, but I'll get us out of this, I promise."

I didn't hear Ashley's response before Bobbie closed the door. For the next couple of hours, they spoke in hushed tones that I couldn't make out through the walls. I thought about getting up and putting my ear to the wall, but I was afraid my unlocked state might be detected if Bobbie came out too quickly for me to get back into bed.

Was I any better off because Bobbie had fewer drugs to move or worse off because she was more desperate? I couldn't be sure. I would have to let it play out. Bobbie would eventually have to go out again to sell the remaining drugs. Ashley was fed up with Bobbie, and she and I had gotten closer. I hoped I could convince her to let me go.

Ashley. This isn't right. You know that. Let me go. I can drive to the hospital and get fixed up, and I promise you'll never hear from me again. That would be Plan A.

Of course, she'd be scared of what Bobbie would do to her when she got home. I'd need a Plan B. *Let's end this nightmare. Take me to the hospital. I'll get fixed up and take you away from all this.*

Plan A: she'd let me go. Plan B: she'd come with me. I liked Plan B better. Was it a bridge too far?

Just then, Ashley yelled from the other room, "I don't believe you. Stay away from me." She bolted out of the bedroom, again slamming the door, and went downstairs. I expected Bobbie to follow, but she remained quiet in the bedroom. It was nice to see her serving her sentence in solitary.

It wasn't until suppertime that either of them stirred. Ashley was in the kitchen clinking dishes when Bobbie walked gingerly downstairs and said, "Ashley, can we talk?"

"No, not right now, Bobbie. Right now, I don't even want you around."

"Okay. How about I go for a walk, and we'll talk when I get back?"

"Go for a walk? In the freezing cold?"

"Yeah. I mean, you don't want me around. I'll go for a walk so you won't even have to see me."

"Okay. Go!"

"I will. I'll do whatever you want."

Ashley didn't respond. The next thing that happened was the side door opened, and a draft of cold air rushed up the back stairs.

Ashley said, "Bobbie, come back," but it was too late. Bobbie was out in the blustery weather, walking to God knows where. I hoped the coyotes in the backyard wouldn't get her.

More dishes clinked, and a pan clunked on the stove. Knives, forks, and spoons tapped the table. The microwave hummed. Down in that kitchen was a woman making supper whose torrent of emotions made her sound like a country band.

After a while, Ashley came upstairs and brought me a bowl of the good soup she had made earlier and another piece of store-bought apple pie—this time heated.

"Are you okay?" I asked.

"I'll be fine," she said and went back downstairs with the lunch dishes that she deposited in the sink. A short while later, her supper dishes went into that same sink—and for all I know, Bobbie's as well. Rather than wash them, she walked upstairs and poked her head into my room.

"You need anything?"

"No," I said, "but—" I blurted out some combination of Plan A and Plan B, although I must admit I got them all jumbled in incomplete sentences with confusing pronouns.

She said no and told me to be quiet—not in the same tone she had told Bobbie, more like if she took in one more thing, she might explode. She gave no explanation. There was no anger in her voice. No fear. No anything. I couldn't read her at all. She went into her bedroom and shut the door, much as the door to her emotions had been shut.

When Bobbie returned, she washed the dishes downstairs, no doubt as penance for her misdeeds. I had done that once or twice with Penny. It takes a lot of penance to melt the ice from a woman's heart. Neither Ashley nor Bobbie picked up my empty dishes. I left my soup bowl on the pie plate with the spoon and fork riding sidesaddle between the two.

I don't know what possessed me, but I grabbed the fork and slipped it under my pillow. Maybe I thought I could MacGyver my escape with it when I got locked up again, or maybe I fantasized that I'd use it in some jujitsu move—Man kills captor with a fork. More likely than not, I would poke myself with it in my sleep.

Bobbie closed up the downstairs and came upstairs. She ignored me completely. No candle was lit in my room. No glass of water. No cuffing me to the bed. She knocked on Ashley's door and asked if she could come in.

I heard nothing from behind their closed door. Either they weren't talking, or they were talking in whispers. What was I to do? Ashley had shot down plans A and B, and I didn't expect Missy to come out of the closet and smite mine enemies.

It looked like the universe was pointing me toward a Plan C. I didn't want to consider it again based on what happened last time, but there it was: escape—quietly get out of bed and make my way downstairs without them hearing me. I had to be cautious. I'd wait until I was sure they had fallen asleep.

When I contemplated my escape—down the stairs, find my car keys, make my way out back to my car, and whiz away—the blood rushed to my face. It was a risky move, and risky moves were not usually in my repertoire.

It's not that I didn't have the courage to do it. It was more that it wasn't the kind of situation I usually found myself in. I have an easy-going personality. Whenever there was a conflict, I was the peacemaker. I could always find a middle ground. I prided myself in being non-confrontational.

Who was I kidding? Why didn't I tell my mother I'll go out with whomever I want? Why didn't I try to win Joanne back? Why didn't I confront Penny when I first saw our marriage was in trouble? Why didn't I tell the Chairman of the Department I didn't want to teach the same boring subjects each semester?

Because I was a coward.

That's why.

I was too much of a coward to get what I wanted and too much of a coward to reject what I didn't.

This magnificent house was here because people had the courage to cross an ocean and face an uncertain future. Even Bobbie had the courage to move into the drug trade. Of course, she had Ashley. What did I have? A broken leg and a broken marriage.

Well, no more. Instead of being the mealy-mouthed professor who never confronted anyone, from now on, I was going to take control of my life— Odysseus bound for Ithaca, Zorba the Greek dancing to my music. That night, I was going to get out of there. This courage thing was infectious. A feeling of euphoria came over me. Maybe it was an aftereffect of the blue pills? Maybe it was what Janis Joplin said, "Freedom's just another word for nothing left to lose."

No matter.

Plan C it was.

I waited until long after the whispers in the next room died out. I stuck the dangling handcuff into the sock on my left foot and eased myself out of bed. I couldn't prevent the squeak of the bedsprings, but by moving slowly, I could keep the volume down.

I fixed the covers so it looked like I was still in the bed, then I grabbed the crutches and ever so slightly placed them ahead of me. I was unable to hop without making a sound. I needed another way.

I eased myself down so I could sit on the floor. I scooched myself forward on my keister like a baby, dragging the crutches along. I moved down the steep stairs, sitting on one step at a time and sliding the crutches along with me. Halfway down, I jammed my finger between the crutch and the stair tread, and the crutches slid the rest of the way down.

I froze in place. Even my breath seemed too loud for the night. I tried to calm the pounding of blood in my ears, my neck, and my chest. No one came out of the bedroom, and I maneuvered my way the rest of the way down.

Now I had to find my keys in the dark. Where would they be? I made my way to the back door and searched for keys on a table. There were none. I circled the room, feeling my way around for any sign of the keys. Nothing. I made my way into the kitchen and felt around the countertops. I came across a flashlight but no keys.

I shined the flashlight all around the kitchen, looking for any sign of the keys, but didn't see any. Penny and I used to keep our keys in the kitchen drawer nearest the side door. It had no keys, nor did any other of the drawers close to the door. Maybe they were in the front parlor where they had some of their secret talks.

Just then, the bedroom door of the Ocean Room opened, and someone was headed downstairs. I scurried to the darkest part of the kitchen and stood straight and stiff as if I were a broom in the corner. Bobbie opened the refrigerator door. I stood six feet behind her, lit up like a convict in a prison spotlight. I had left my crutches leaning on the kitchen table right behind her. She took out some orange juice, drank from the bottle, and replaced it in the fridge. The room went dark again when she closed the door and went back upstairs.

I stood there for a long time before I dared move again. When I did, I hopped into the parlor. There across the couch was Bobbie's coat. I reached into the pocket and found her car keys. Mine were not in the other pocket, and no other jackets were in view.

I put on her coat and made my way to my crutches and the back door. When I got there, I saw the ground was covered with a dusting of fresh snow, and my good foot was only covered with a wool sock. No boots were in sight but forget it. I just wanted to get out of there.

I opened the back door, and the wind whistled in a blast of cold air. I imagined it drafting its way up the back stairs. I hoped Bobbie closed the bedroom door when she went back to sleep. Too late to worry about that now. I swung my way through the doorway and shut the door behind me as fast as I could.

At first, the snow-covered porch felt cold through my sock, but by the time I sat on the top step, the sock was soaked. I maneuvered my way down the porch stairs, hands on one step, fanny on the next, crutches following. Now, my foot was freezing, and my hands were numb. A strong wind was howling, and I had no scarf and no hat. I hobbled my way back to Bobbie's car. Her SUV was old enough to require a key to unlock it rather than using a fob. I was just as glad. I wouldn't want a high-pitched beep to tip off anyone upstairs.

I tried to place the key in the lock, but it was hard to get it right in the dark, and the wind seemed to be howling even harder than when I first came out. The key slipped through my frost-bitten hand into the snow. I reached down and picked it up. I cast the crutches aside and made one focused attempt to feel the door lock with one hand and insert the key with the other.

I unlocked the door and hopped back to let myself in. A force hit me from behind, and I bounced off the side of the car before ending up on the ground.

Bobbie was on top of me.

"Trustworthy, my ass! I should leave you behind the shed. You can freeze to death, and the animals will pick your bones clean."

Thoughts were swirling around my head. My mind was already driving the SUV away, and yet my body was pinned under Bobbie in the cold snow. It took me a second to realize everything had changed. She was talking death and animals picking my bones. I was too scared to do anything but cower there on the ground.

I reverted to the arguments I had been giving all along. "No, Bobbie. I'm not going to tell. Please. I just want to get out of here."

"I can't take any more trouble. Not from you. Not from anyone." Bobbie was out of control.

Thank God, Ashley's voice called out from the back door. "Bring him in. You're both going to freeze out there."

Bobbie grabbed me by the collar of her coat and brought me to my feet—my foot. She tried to take me back to the house, but there was no way I could move without the crutches. She let go of me to pick up the crutches, and I just stood there like a frightened flamingo. She threw one of the crutches away. The other got tucked under my left arm. She helped me stay upright with a hammer-lock on my right arm—a far cry from Ashley's buddy walk. I hobbled ahead of her, and when I slipped and fell, she righted me with a hard lift and a knee in my side.

Bobbie made sure the bed lock was secured this time. Ashley rubbed my bare foot between her hands and put a dry sock on me.

"Why was he unlocked?" The dominant Bobbie was back.

"I just forgot." Ashley fell back into her submissive groove.

I remained speechless. Any words I uttered would be like throwing a match onto a gasoline-soaked bed.

THE GRAB

A *rap rap rap* invaded my dreams. I ignored it in favor of sleep. It returned, *rap rap rap rap rap,* faster than before, more raps in the same amount of time, almost the rhythm of a woodpecker. The wind howled outside. No self-respecting woodpecker would be out in weather like this. I opened my eyes. They didn't want to open. It was morning. Friday already. The light filtering through the shades was too bright, and the night had been too awful.

I had taken a blue pill after Bobbie and Ashley locked me in and went to sleep. I wasn't seeking euphoria; I was seeking numbness. I wanted to be anywhere but on this earth. I got my wish. Not what I expected. On my journey through the cosmos, I ran into an unseen veil that closed around me like a fish in a net. It dragged me into a black hole.

All the ghosts of my past were waiting. They came at me, a coordinated attack, one after the other, always from my blind side.

The first started as a pinprick of light in the darkness behind me. When it got closer, it got brighter. I started running up a set of stairs—the stairs in Joanne's hallway. A freight train behind me was gaining on me. The faster I ran, the more the stairs moved downward like an escalator beneath my feet.

Joanne stood at the top of the stairs with her new boyfriend, laughing like funhouse ghouls. I didn't want to reach them, but I couldn't stop running for fear the train would catch me. When it did, all I could do was lie still between the tracks and hope that its undercarriage didn't catch an article of clothing or a twitch of a limb.

When the train passed, I again found myself in the black void. I rose to my feet and spotted Penny. She was standing in her wedding dress. The void filled with our family and friends in church. Penny floated down the aisle toward me. I was so relieved to see her greet me with the same wide smile and a big "Hi" that she did on our wedding day—but she didn't stop.

She floated right by me and out the side door of the church.

I looked back at our family and friends in the pews, and Penny was again standing at the rear of the church. She floated down the aisle toward me, faster this time, and made the same loop over and over again, each time faster and faster, until her motion was just a blur of white light surrounding me.

I ran out of the church into the street. The trash collectors were picking up our barrels. They dumped the *Les Miz* poster in the back of the truck and took off. I chased them down the street, but they disappeared into the void.

There was nothing left to do but stare into the blackness. Time has no place in a void. The world could be stopped or recklessly spinning—it makes no difference.

Church bells started ringing. I turned and looked up. The bell tower stood against a round glow in the darkness. Ashley was in the tower, striking the bell with her skillet. Bong. Bong. Bong. With each strike, the sound became more deafening.

I began to run but couldn't outrun blackness. It was as if I were on a treadmill going nowhere. Faster and faster until exhaustion forced me to lay on the ground. It was cold under my back, and then a heavy beam cracked my leg. When it bounced upward, the bone re-formed into a whole again. The beam came back down. Another crack, bounce, and reconstitution of the bone. Crack-bounce, crack-bounce. I was experiencing the break of my leg again and again. The ice pick was thrust into my flesh and extracted with every bounce.

The void was my Groundhog Day movie. Not only couldn't I get out, but also the groundhog was getting beat up.

Then the ghosts arrived.

A wailing sound came from inside the locked closet. At first, I thought it was Missy mourning her son or her husband, but no, her lament was over my night with Ashley.

"Mend thy lascivious ways" was her war cry. "Mend thy lascivious ways." Hers wasn't the only voice in the room.

Behind me, the Indian from the hut was chanting a *Hiy-ya-ya-ya* while shaking a corn husk at me and pow-wow dancing in a circle around me. On the other side of the circle, a black Kentucky witch doctor was rattling hoodoo bones and mouthing some devil-incantation in my direction. All around the circle, ghoulish figures with faces half-melted like wax or heads with goat snouts and beards or oversized teeth protruding from lipless mouths danced with the Indian and the witch doctor. I tried to escape, but at every turn, I saw Bobbie with a carving knife ready to chop me up and feed me to the animals behind the shed.

Everything started spinning as if I were trapped in a tornado. The last thing I remembered was the blurred images of Joanne, Penny, and Ashley flying by me before a merciful god rendered me unconscious.

The sleep that came was more like a grave than a bed. And now even that fortuitous sleep was being challenged.

Rap rap rap rap, continuous now, louder, demanding a response.

Bobbie raced out of the Ocean Room to the top of the back stairs. Ashley was right behind her.

"Who is it? Can you see who it is?"

"No, It's a man at the side door."

"What are we going to do?"

Rap rap rap rap rap.

"I don't know. He sounds determined."

"Bobbie! Are you in there?" The intruder stopped knocking and yelled Bobbie's name.

"It's Eddie."

Bobbie ran down the stairs and opened the door.

"Eddie, come inside. Quick. What are you doing here?"

"I told you I had a connection. I talked to the Captain; he's interested in buying your whole stash."

"Let's go in the other room and talk. Where's your car?"

"Right there."

"You have to bring it around to the back of the house. I'll meet you at the back door."

Eddie went back outside, and Bobbie ran upstairs to Ashley.

"Make us some coffee?"

"Sure," and Ashley went down.

Bobbie popped her head into my room and said, "So help me, if you make one peep, you're a dead man."

Then she ran downstairs to meet Eddie at the back door.

She introduced Eddie to Ashley. They had been high school buddies. Hung out together a lot. Old friends talk like they have never been apart. Eddie and Bobbie went into the front parlor while Ashley banged around in the kitchen.

I didn't dare make a move. I had no idea what was happening except what I heard when Eddie first came in. Maybe Bobbie was finally going to sell what was left of her stash and get out of debt with the Tampa loan sharks. I would soon learn my fate.

They talked for a long time. Ashley snuck a cup of coffee and a piece of toast up to me and pleaded with me to stay quiet.

When Eddie left, he said, "Great meeting you, Ashley."

"Likewise, Eddie."

"I hope to see you again," and he was out the back door.

"Ashley, we're saved. I can sell the rest of the stuff to Eddie's contact, and we can go home in the morning. Pack our stuff. We're getting out of here."

"What about him?"

"Who?"

"Cliff. When are we going to let him go?"

"Let's go to the other room."

They headed to the front parlor.

This was a conversation I had to hear. Did I dare? What if I got caught again? Big deal. What's she going to do, kill me? My misbehavior is her problem more than it's my problem. This courage thing was like a drug. I was high on it.

I popped the pineapple off the top of the bedpost and freed myself. I swiveled my broken leg off the bed. My broken leg was my problem, not hers. What was I doing? Courage is the lie we tell ourselves to justify our stupidity. Still, I had to know what they were saying. That wasn't stupid. Was it?

I made my way as quickly as I could without making any noise to the Captain's Room. Bobbie was in the middle of explaining Eddie's pedigree to Ashley. I lay down on the floor and listened through the grate.

"The fishing industry is going broke. All that regulation on the little guys while the big, foreign ships harvest all the fish. Anyway, Eddie knows this captain who was not only surviving but flourishing. Turns out he's distributing more than fish all the way from Block Island to Portsmouth, New Hampshire. Eddie's reputation preceded him, and he crews for this guy a lot. I told Eddie what we had, and he talked to the guy.

He said if I had what I said I had, he'd buy the whole kit and kaboodle—and he'd give me the full 100K. I told Eddie I already sold 50K. He said that was probably okay. I think it may have made him even more eager. Turns out the guy will be leaving from Stage Harbor tonight. If I bring the stuff, he'll have the money. Ashley, we can leave for Florida in the morning!"

"That's great. What about Cliff?"

"I'm still working on that."

"What do you mean working on it? What's to work on? We'll drop him off at the Cape Cod Hospital on our way back to Florida."

"We can't do that."

"Why not?"

"He'll call the cops. We wouldn't get as far as Connecticut before—"

"No, I talked to him. His story is as desperate as ours. He actually came down here to commit suicide. He was going to throw himself into the ocean. He knows what it's like to have everyone you care about betray you. He's sympathetic to our troubles. He is, Bobbie. He won't tell anyone anything."

"You're being naïve again. He tried to escape again last night."

"I know, but that's because he doesn't trust us."

"Well, I don't trust him."

"You don't have to trust him. Trust me this time. I'm sure about this."

"Yeah, like you were sure of your co-workers . . . and your sisters?"

"That's not fair."

"What's not fair is what they all did to us."

"But what are you going to do to him?"

Bobbie whispered something, but I couldn't hear it.

"No, you can't! Ashley screamed.

"Hold your voice down."

The two of them now spoke in whispers. I couldn't make out the words, but it was clear they were arguing. Come on, Ashley, assert yourself. Bobbie, Bobbie, Bobbie, haven't you heard the expression, *happy wife, happy life?*

Bobbie started talking in a calm voice. "Don't you see? It's perfect. He was going to commit suicide anyway. He probably even left a note somewhere."

"But he doesn't want to now. He just wants to get to the hospital and then go home."

"Ashley, haven't you learned your lesson? If we don't take care of ourselves, no one is going to take care of us."

"I don't care. I'll throw the drugs out first. I'll have no part of murder."

Murder! Holy shit. That word coming out of Ashley's mouth made it seem real.

"You won't have to. When I bring the stuff to the fisherman at midnight, you give him a pill. When I get back—"

She kept talking, but I stopped listening. I had to think fast. She was going to sell the drugs to the fisherman and then kill me. The duffel bag was staring me in the face.

I heard her say, "—the Monomoy Wildlife Refuge."

I had been there. A high cliff overlooked the ocean between the deserted refuge and Monomoy Island. That's where she was going to hurl my drugged body into the icy waters.

Bobbie was still talking when I grabbed the duffel bag.

"We'll be free and clear then and put all this behind us."

I crawled back to the Author's Room and squeezed under the bed. I lifted the board with a knot hole and stuffed the two remaining bags of blue pills and the one bag of LSD vials inside. Then I shimmied out and made my way to the key hanging on a nail behind the bureau. I placed the empty duffel bag on the floor behind Missy's dress form, locked the door, and returned the key. By the time I got back into bed and rewickered my leash, no one was the wiser, but I had crossed the Rubicon.

No drugs, no sale, no death. That stash was my only bargaining chip.

They went on for about an hour; then they moved back to the kitchen, where they said very little.

Had they made a decision?

Were they just at an impasse?

The sun had passed over the top of the house, and my stomach was growling. I figured it was about 2:00—ten hours to the drop off with the fisherman.

Ashley came upstairs with a sandwich and a soda. That's what they were doing in the kitchen, having lunch. If this was my last meal, it wasn't what I'd call gourmet. Ham and cheese.

I said to Ashley, "I heard Bobbie say she sold the merchandise."

"Yes." Her answer seemed tentative, like she wanted to know how much else I heard.

I played dumb.

"That's good news. I'm glad for you."

She gave a pained smile.

"Did you ask Bobbie if I could have another blue pill?"

Her answer came swiftly, "No more blue pills."

I was glad she gave me that answer. It meant she hadn't given in to Bobbie's Monomoy plan.

"Do you really need one?" Bobbie surprised us both at the bedroom door. She walked into the room and checked my ankle restraints like she was performing a routine inspection in a meat packing plant. She repeated, "Do you need one?"

"I thought I did, but it seems to be better now."

Ashley chimed in, "He doesn't need them anymore; besides, they can be addictive."

"See how it goes. If you need one, you can have it. No sense in being miserable."

I looked at Ashley. She was glaring at Bobbie.

"We'll see," she said, and she left the room, heading down the corridor.

Was she going to the Captain's Room? Would she notice that the duffel bag was missing? We heard nothing from her.

Bobbie said, "Don't worry about it. If you need a pill, I'll get it for you. Eat up. It's a good sandwich. I still have half of mine waiting downstairs." With that, she went downstairs.

Ashley came back by the Author's Room, and she said, "Don't say anything!"

Then she went downstairs.

They argued in hushed tones. I could only make out an occasional word or snatches of phrases: *later, home free, times running out, Godsend, not leaving this house, pack our stuff.*

I heard *hypo-something.* At first, I thought it was *hypodermic,* but then, when I thought about it, it was probably *hypothermia.* In that freezing water, I'd be dead in—I didn't know about hypothermia, but I didn't want to learn.

I began to formulate my plan. When Bobbie discovered the drugs were gone, I'd tell her that they were hidden in the eaves of the house where she would never find them. Maybe I'd show her the hidden ladder and the hatch into the attic. She could crawl around for days, looking in all the crevices inside those eaves. She had no option but to listen to my demands.

When Ashley drives me to the hospital, I'll tell her where they are. Otherwise, you will lose the deal. Take it or leave it.

Things were quiet downstairs. Either they weren't talking, or they were talking so softly I couldn't hear them. For a while, I thought maybe they went out, but then I heard someone knock something over downstairs. The minutes ticked by slowly. My pulse was racing. I could feel sweat accumulating on my brow.

Maybe I should give her the drugs just to show my trustworthiness. After all, if I could have scuttled the deal and I didn't, that should count for something. Bobbie wasn't a murderer. She was just desperate.

But desperate people do desperate things. I was proof of that. What was that book I once read? *When Bad Things Happen to Good People.* There should be a sequel. *When Good People Do Bad*

Things. I didn't want to write that book. I certainly didn't want to be the one to whom good people do bad things.

My sandwich sat untouched in the dish. I couldn't eat. My insides were knotted in my gullet. Not only had I crossed the Rubicon, but also I was threatening Rome itself. My fate was in the hands of the gods. The light in the bedroom faded as if the gods were signaling an impending disaster.

It was just dusk—not the gods. I had to stay logical and focused. The Chatham sun fell below the treetops behind the house. It was likely getting near five o'clock. Sometime between now and midnight, Bobbie would discover the drugs were missing.

I had to get my act together, rehearse my words. How I played it would mean the difference between disaster and freedom. Freedom. Freedom. I could hear Janice Joplin belting out the word. Wait. It was Aretha. Why did I think it was Janice? I get my women so mixed up.

I'd calmly say, "I have your drugs. If you want them back—"

No, first I should say, "You'll never find them," just to establish the new rules.

Then I'd say, "If you kill me, you will never get your drugs." I shouldn't use the word *kill.* A better word would be *hurt.* Yeah, "If you hurt me, you'll never get your drugs."

Of course, that wasn't true. If she hurt me, that was the best way for her to get them. A coward can't take pain. What was I talking about? If I gave her the drugs, I'd be signing my own death warrant.

The room grew darker. How many times had I ventured across the street to watch the sky grow dimmer until the last light of day blinked off, merging the sky and the ocean into a single black canvas dotted above with stars and below with whitecaps? It wouldn't be long now before I learned my fate.

I memorized my words—*You'll never find them. If you hurt me, you will never get them.* I rehearsed them. I had the words down straight, but I might not ever get to say them. Bobbie might kill me first. Desperate people. Desperate things.

The room had become total darkness.

Footsteps rose on the stairs along with the flicker of candlelight. It was Ashley come to light the candle in my room and give me a more substantial supper—a hamburger and home fries—a last meal I might have ordered.

"Ashley," I whispered, "no matter what happens tonight, you have to know that all I want is to leave here. I want you and Bobbie to get through this all right. I just want my freedom. You understand that, don't you?"

"I do," she said in a hushed tone.

"Then, you can't let Bobbie do anything bad to me. You won't, will you?"

"You need to rest now. It will all be over tonight."

"No, I just want to get out of here."

"I have to go back downstairs."

She turned to leave, then she stopped and looked back.

"Do you want a blue pill?"

CHAPTER ELEVEN

BECKY SUE

Midnight was approaching. Bobbie was going to kill me. Ashley wasn't going to be able to stop her. Now, what was I going to do? Wait, I forgot. I had the upper hand. The words. What were the words I was going to say? I needed to calm down, to stay calm.

I moved my crutches closer to the headboard. If I had to, I could use one to defend myself. Who was I kidding? With my one good leg shackled to the bedpost, I would soon be the one taking the beating.

I had only one card to play—the hidden drugs.

Ashley came upstairs, and I asked her what time it was. She said it was 10:30.

"What's going to happen?" I asked.

"Bobbie's going to sell the drugs tonight." She said.

"No, I mean, when are you going to let me go?"

"We're still talking about that. We haven't decided yet."

"Decided what?"

"I can't talk about that right now. Just stay calm."

She went back downstairs, and again, they spoke in whispers. Bobbie shouted, "I don't have time for that right now. I have to bring the merchandise to Stage Harbor."

She came bounding up the stairs and went into the Captain's Room, where she had stored the drugs that I stole.

"Jesus Christ!" she bellowed.

She'd be on me in seconds. *I have your drugs.* No, that shouldn't be the first thing I say. *Kill me, and you'll never find them.* Don't use the word *kill.* I forgot everything I rehearsed.

Bobbie raced down the corridor toward my room. I tensed all my muscles, but she ran right past and down the stairs. She jumped the last few stairs and landed with a thud in the kitchen.

"You bitch! What did you do?"

"Bobbie, what do you want? You're scaring me." Ashley sounded confused.

"What did you do with the drugs? I know you took them. What did you do with them?"

"I didn't take them." Ashley's voice seemed to be retreating into a corner of the kitchen.

"Don't lie to me." Bobbie was yelling at football-stadium volume. "Just to protect him? What about me? What about all the trouble I'm in? What did you do with the stuff?"

"I didn't—"

Bobbie kept repeating it: "What did you do with the stuff?"

Ashley yelled, "Let go of me!"

I heard a scuffle. Ashley's voice twisted, "Le-et go of me-e. You bastard. Leave me al—"

A loud slap cut off her words, and Bobbie screeched, "You betrayed me."

A jumble of sounds followed, as if she hit the floor to escape another blow or as if Bobbie wrestled her down. Ashley sobbed, "What's wrong with you?"

"If I don't show up in an hour, we're toast. Where's the stuff?"

"I didn't take them, I tell you."

"Don't lie to me."

"Stop! Stop! You're hurting me."

I yelled down, "I took the drugs!"

The commotion downstairs came to a halt. I held my breath. The only sound was Ashley whimpering.

Like a crack of thunder, Bobbie's heavy boots hit the stairs, and she came bounding up.

She burst into the darkened room with her eyes flashing in the candlelight like one of those night shots of coyote wolves that inhabit the Cape. In a second, she had her hands around my throat. "Where's my stuff?"

I pushed her arms back to take a breath and struggled to give a response. "I'll tell you if you stop choking me."

"Talk." She looked more like she wanted to kill than talk.

"I took them—for insurance. Let Ashley drive me to the hospital, then I'll tell you."

"Bullshit. I'll find them. They didn't go very far."

"You'll never find them. I guarantee that. This house has a thousand places to hide stuff." I used my best poker face.

She pointed at me, and the words came out as if they were being forced through a grinder: "Where are they? Where's the stuff?"

She looked under the bed. Pulled the drawers out of the bureaus, spilled the contents, and threw them to the floor. She looked around the room like a madwoman.

I searched my gut for the courage I was pretending to have and said, "You let me go, and I will tell you where everything is."

She didn't pay me any attention. She pulled the quilt cover off the bed, then yanked the top sheet out of my clinging hands. I was completely exposed. She rifled through the covers on the floor, looking for the bags of drugs. When she found nothing, she grabbed one of my two pillows and yanked the pillowcase off. The handful of blue pills I had previously stolen for my recreation fell to the floor.

She hit me with a pillow and said, "You son of a bitch. Where are the rest of them?"

"Take me to the hospital, and I'll—"

She punched me in the gut. I tried to curl into a ball, but my left leg was restrained, and my right wouldn't bend with the splint. I drew my elbows in to protect my stomach from a second punch that was cocked and ready to fire. She diverted it into a roundhouse blow to the left side of my face. The pain drove a loud ouch out of my mouth. I brought one arm over my face while the other continued to protect my midsection.

Ashley yelled from the bottom of the stairs, "Bobbie, what are you doing?" She didn't come up. Was she scared? Bleeding? I had no idea. I was on my own.

Bobbie grabbed my arms and shook me. "Where's my stuff?"

I looked to the closet as if Missy was going to bust out, breathing fire and revenge.

Bobbie saw my glance and went to the closet. It was locked.

"Where's the key?"

"There IS no key. That closet's been locked ever since I've been coming here."

She was convinced I was lying, and the duffel bag of drugs was in the closet. And she was right about the duffel bag. I was proud of myself for throwing her onto the scent of an empty bag.

She grabbed my crutch and pointed at me like she was going to jam it into my neck or head.

I set my arms like a karate master preparing to deflect an attack. Kung Fooey Louie.

"Where's the key?" She shouted.

"Take me to the hospital."

She pulled the crutch way back like she was about to thrust. Maybe she hesitated because my hand jive frightened her. More like she thought she might kill me, and there was no return for her in that. I was about to tell her where the key was when she spun around and used the crutch as a battering ram against the closet door. She broke through one of the wood panels on the right side. Then she broke through the panel on the left, but the slab between panels would not yield to her battering.

"I'll show you," she said, and she raced down the back stairs. I didn't know if she was talking to me or the door. If she was talking to the door, I figured she'd come back up with a sledge-hammer. Instead, she came back up with a large chef's knife. She was talking to me.

She clasped the knife in both hands and raised her arms like the stab was going to run right through me into the bed. I reached under the remaining pillow for the fork. It was nowhere to be found.

I tried to roll out of her way, but the pain in my leg overtook me. I grabbed my leg and screamed. Now Bobbie knew exactly how and where to hurt me.

She dropped the knife on the floor and grabbed the foot of my broken leg—the toeless sneaker that Ashley had bound up.

Pain flooded me as if the skin on the left side of my body had been pinched by a giant tool.

I screamed and rose high off the bed. Blue and purple shapes filled my vision while the bedsprings squealed like a subway train on a curve.

Ashley yelled up, "Bobbie! Stop!"

Bobbie then picked up the knife and jabbed the point against my private parts. With one leg hog-tied to the bedpost and the other in a splint, my manhood was about to be guillotined. I diverted her attention toward my splinted leg and yelled, "My leg is broken. My leg—it hurts!"

It didn't work. She kept her attention on my crotch. "Tell me where the keys are, or I'll turn you into a tunic." She meant eunuch. It was no time to correct her.

"Behind the bureau. It's on a nail behind the bureau."

The contest was over. She had won.

She laid the knife on the bureau and pulled it out to find the keys. The keys weren't going to do her any good. The duffel bag in the closet was empty. I had very little time to plan my next move. What next move? I was out of ideas.

Ashley appeared. She took the knife and threw it down into the kitchen.

Bobbie was concentrating on getting the key in the lock.

Ashley grabbed her arm. "Bobbie! Stop! Stop it! This is crazy."

The key fell to the floor. Bobbie retrieved it and a dagger-like remnant of the splintered door that she pointed at Ashley. "Get out of here. Go downstairs."

Ashley backed away.

Bobbie unlocked what was left of the closet door and pulled it open so fast that it banged the wall. Then she stepped inside. Candlelight from the room cast moving shadows of her arms swinging in and out of the shelves, her feet sweeping left and right—erratic movements that indicated her rational mind had abandoned her.

She found the duffel bag on the floor behind Missy's dress form and yanked it up. Bobbie, the bag, and Missy's form stumbled backward out of the closet, landing on the floor at the foot of the bed. Bobbie let out a scream of frustration.

She untangled herself from Missy and lifted the bag onto the bed. I could see that she already figured it was empty. Once she started to unzip, she tore it open the rest of the way.

"They're not in there," I shouted. "Take me to the hospital, and I'll tell you."

She got up and came around to the side of the bed. "You'll tell me now!"

With that, she grabbed my foot, and I called out, "Stop!"

Ashley came forward and slowly inserted herself between me and Bobbie. "Stop. Bobbie," she said calmly. She coaxed Bobbie's hand off of me. "Let me talk to Cliff. He'll tell me."

I'd tell her. I'd tell her anything. Where the drugs were, for sure. How I cared about her, although now was not a good time. Not with Bobbie listening.

Ashley coaxed Bobbie to step back. She took two steps and then twitched like she was going to lurch forward. Ashley stroked her face. "No, Bobbie. Stop. He'll tell me. Just wait. Be patient." She patted Bobbie's shoulders like she was molding a sand castle to stand on its own.

Then she turned to me. One of her cheeks was pink; the other glowed red, no doubt from the slap. She whispered, "Cliff, please tell me where it is."

I whispered back, "I can't, Ash. If I tell you, she'll kill me."

"No, she won't. She's not like that. I won't let her. Look, she has to deliver the stuff. If you promise me you won't go to the police, I will help you to your car and let you go."

"Will you come with me?"

"Please, Cliff. Tell me where the stuff is. I'll do whatever you want after."

It took me a minute to process. Did she mean let me go or come with me? Neither sat well with Bobbie. She burst forward and yelled. "Tell me!"

She went for my foot again. I screamed in pain.

Ashley yelled, "Noooo," and jumped on Bobbie. She wrapped herself around Bobbie like a misplaced piggyback. Bobbie spun around, and Ashley hit the wall and floor hard.

Bobbie looked down at her with her arms outstretched. "I'm sorry. I'm sorry." Then she looked back at me. I don't know whether she was saying, "Look what you made me do," or "Help me."

I gave her nothing back but defiance. Captain Courageous!

She squatted down over Ashley. "Don't you see? We're in deep shit. If I don't show, we're dead meat."

She rose up and attempted to help Ashley to her feet, but instead, got pushed back with a foot in the chest.

Bobbie moved toward her like a grizzly threatening on its hind legs. Ashley scrambled toward the back stairs and scurried down. Bobbie took a step back and turned her attention to me. A hateful look. Without Ashley, my goose was cooked.

"You'll tell me where they are, or I swear I will twist your goddamn leg off."

She moved slowly toward me, looking straight into my eyes. What I saw in hers was the devil's stare and the hell I was about to enter. I recoiled and felt the cold metal of the fork under the remaining pillow.

She laid her hand on my foot, never breaking eye contact.

"Tell me now or else!" She gave it a threatening twist.

I yelled, "Ow? Jesus, Bobbie, that hurt. I'll tell you! I'll tell you. Just promise to let me go." I grasped the fork like an ice pick.

"I'll promise shit. And you'll tell me." She took a firm grip on my sneakered foot. "So help me, God!" She looked as if her hand was on the doomsday machine about to end the world.

"Don't!" I added a long, weepy "Pleeee-ease don't." I'd thrust the fork into her skull, or her eye, or her neck. Whatever opportunity presented itself.

She had the devil's stare in her eyes, and with one blow of my weapon, I was ready to join her in Hell. *Smite thine enemies.*

Her face became distorted by a demonic smile—teeth like fangs, eyes bulging like a squeeze toy, pigtails snaking across her cheeks. She knew she had broken me, and she was gloating over it.

I looked up at her through a lens of tears, searching for some sign of humanity in her eyes before I plunged my forked dagger deep into one of them. My blurred vision caught a flicker of blonde moving behind her. A loud *clunk* rang out, and Bobbie's head jerked forward. She fell across my legs, and everything went quiet.

Ashley stood in my field of view, holding the same skillet that had done me in.

Except for the tears, Ashley remained still, like a statue of a Greek goddess holding a sacred scroll.

I said, "Ashley, unlock me."

She didn't move.

"Ashley!"

She looked down at Bobbie and over at me. Such despair. Someone in a war zone wandering around after a bombing.

"Ashley, unlock me."

Her gaze seemed vacant. "It's over." Her words came out monotone, disconnected. "What are we going to do now?"

"Let's just leave. You and me, Ash. We'll go together."

She didn't answer. She closed her eyes, furrowed her brow, and tilted her head. "No," she said as if the *no* was the answer to her internal dialog. When her eyes opened, they were different, clearer. "I can't just leave Bobbie. The loan sharks. They'll kill her. The sea captain. He could be dangerous, too."

She was determined to save Bobbie.

I took hold of her shoulders. "Then there's only one thing to do."

"What?"

"Unlock me, and I'll tell you," A crazy plan formed in the back of my head. I was not only going to save myself, but I was going to save Ashley—and Bobbie—all at the same time. The plan took shape in the seconds it took for her to unlock me. Crazy, but it could work.

When I tried to extricate myself from Bobbie's body lying across my legs, she fell to the floor. She hit with a muffled thud like a barbell wrapped in a sack of blankets.

Ashley knelt next to her and felt her pulse. I stood up, braced by the footboard and pineapple post.

"Help me get Bobbie onto the bed," she said.

She bear-hugged Bobbie as she had me, and I helped swing Bobbie's legs onto the bed. Bobbi was now lying right where I was minutes before.

"What have I done?" Ashley was in shock. "We're ruined. It's almost midnight."

I spun Ashley around.

"It's not too late."

"Huh?"

"Do you know the fisherman's name?"

"Atkins. Captain Cecil Atkins."

"Perfect. We'll go to the harbor and make the deal. You and me. That takes care of those guys. Then we'll come back here with the money and give it to Bobbie. That will take care of the loan sharks in Florida."

"You and me?"

"Yes. By the time Bobbie wakes up, it'll be over."

"She'll be furious."

"No. Don't you see, it's the solution we've been hoping for. Bobbie will have her money to pay off the Florida loan sharks, and I will be implicated."

"I'll be implicated, too."

"True. But once I'm implicated, Bobbie can let me go without any fear that I'll go to the cops, and I can go get my leg fixed. You'll have to decide what you want to do after that."

I could see her wondering what I meant by that. I had my idea of what she should do, where she should go, and with whom, but this wasn't the time to think about all that. We had to act right away.

Ashley didn't seem to comprehend everything I was telling her. Hell, I wasn't sure if I did. I fished the handcuff keys out of Bobbie's pocket and locked one set of cuffs from her limp wrist to the thick wire of the bed spring and one set from her ankle to the bedpost cuff.

"But where are the drugs?" Ashley seemed to be catching up to me.

I lowered myself to the floor and slid under the bed. From the hidden compartment, I took out the first bag of blue pills and handed them out.

"Put these into the duffel bag,"

I handed her the rest of the pills and the vials of LSD.

Small clouds of glowing fog surrounded the few streetlights on the forest-lined road to Stage Harbor. Our headlights alternately pushed through patches of fog and shone far into the night. We parked off the road in a dark notch in the tree line.

It wasn't hard to find Atkins on this cold winter night. Only one boat sat next to the dock with its motor idling and its interior lights on. We approached cautiously. The name painted across the back of the boat was Becky Sue. The crunch of feet and crutches on the snow was too soft to be heard over the running engine.

When we suddenly appeared out of the darkness, a big guy, tough-looking, with a few days of beard on his face and many years of wear on his face, stepped to the boat rail. He pulled his stocking cap down past his ears and picked up a pole with a mean-looking hook at the end.

"What d'ya want?"

"Are you Cecil Atkins?" Ashley asked.

"Who wants to know?"

"Bobbie sent us. We have something for Captain Atkins."

He looked us up and down.

"Stay put." He pointed the business end of the hook at us. I wasn't going to move.

Toward the front of the boat, a cabin sat one level above us, all lit up and enclosed in glass. It housed the ship's wheel and all kinds of electronic equipment, but no one was in it. He stepped under that cabin and opened a door to what looked like a galley below deck.

"Cap'n! There's someone here."

A man dressed in a pea coat and a faded Red Sox baseball cap came out. He had a perfectly groomed sea captain's beard and a ruddy complexion. His eyes sized us up with a look that reminded me of one of those fluoroscopes that sees right through you in the hospital.

"What can I do for you?"

"Are you Cecil Atkins?"

"Maybe. Who are you?"

"We're here for Bobbie. We have something for you."

"I don't know any Bobbie."

Ashley said, "Eddie set it up. Eddie Wheatley. He told us to be here at midnight."

"Who's us?"

"I'm Ashley. This here is Cliff. Bobbie couldn't make it, so Cliff came with me."

"I got a crew." He nodded in Hookman's direction. "Besides, I'm not hiring women or one-legged sailors."

I stepped forward on the dock and whispered, "We're not here to go fishing. We're selling, and I heard you're buying." I was channeling Humphrey Bogart.

He whispered back, "You got the wrong idea, pal. I'm going fishing, and if I don't leave in the next few minutes, I'm not going to make it through Muskeeget Channel before the tide changes."

He stepped away and said to his crew member, "Cast off, Poke." Then he headed back to the wheelhouse. Poke jumped onto the dock and released the lines at the back and front of the boat, then jumped back aboard. The Captain was opening the door to the wheelhouse when I hooked my crutch onto the rail of the boat.

"Wait! I said. "We came all his way to make a deal, and we will make it."

Poke lifted his lance and hooked my crutch.

"The only thing you're going to make is a splash in the water if you don't get out of here."

I recovered my crutch, and by this time, Captain Atkins had put the engine in gear and motored away from the dock.

I looked at Ashley and said, "I'm sorry."

She said, "Let's go." She carried the duffel bag, and I trailed behind on my crutches.

"When we got back inside the car, I said, "I think he got suspicious because he didn't know who we were. Maybe he figured we were cops or something. I'm not sure what to do next."

Ashley started the car and said, "I am."

She drove off into the night.

CHAPTER TWELVE
EDDIE MY LOVE

When we got back to Chatham House, it was past dawn. My outlook on the future had improved markedly. The part that gave me the most hope was how Ashley acted when she brought me into the Cape Cod Hospital Emergency Room.

When we left the Captain, we followed route 28 to Hyannis. The hospital was easy to find.

"Here we are," She said. "It's up to you how you handle it."

No preconditions.

She dropped me off at the door and said she'd park the car and come in. The ER was pretty much deserted at that hour of the night. A young woman with too many tattoos and unkempt hair was asleep on her boyfriend's shoulder. They both looked malnourished. A family of four sat together on the far side of the waiting room, whispering in Spanish. The woman's hand was wrapped in a bloody towel, and her husband was consoling her while he held his little girl and another child slept on the bench next to him.

I told the admitting nurse that a couple of days ago, I was chipping the ice off our back stairs with an ice pick and lost my footing. Took a terrible fall. My leg broke when I got tangled in the railing, and the ice pick landed in my thigh. My wife used to be a nurse. We were snowed in, so she got me inside, dressed the wound, and put the makeshift brace on my leg. She took good care of me until we could get plowed out, and here we were.

Ashley did take good care of me. Despite the primitive conditions at the house and Bobbie's wrath toward me, the doc said my tibia fracture was non-displaced, and with the proper cast he put on, I should be okay again in four to five months. Maybe I'd need some physical therapy, but the prognosis for a return to normal was pretty good.

What the doc had no way of knowing was that with Bobbie cuffed to the bed in Chatham, the prognosis for a return to normal was anything but good.

When we entered through the back door, the house was quiet. Was Bobbie even still up there? I had imagined her waking up in a frenzy and trying in vain to get loose. When I was cuffed to the bed, I eventually quit trying, but Bobbie was of a different temperament. I didn't picture her giving up. Maybe she was up there out of energy, like a dog that had exhausted itself chasing its tail.

"Ashley, is that you?" Bobbie's voice was quiet and restrained.

Maybe she just realized the error of her ways and was coming to Ashley profoundly sorry for everything she had done.

"Ashley?" Her voice was a little louder but still humble.

Ashley removed her coat and walked to the bottom of the stairs. "Bobbie. I'm coming up." She signaled to me to stay behind, paused a moment, took a long deep breath, and proceeded up the stairs—not too fast, not slow either, more like a deliberate walk on stage to deliver a speech.

"Bobbie, I have something to say to you."

"Ashley, let me loose. I'm sorr—"

"Bobbie, I have something to say, and I don't want you to say another word, or I'll leave here just like I left Kentucky."

"But—"

"Not a word!" Ashley spoke with judicial authority, and Bobbie went silent.

She continued, "You remember that night I left my Daddy, and he never saw me again? Well, that's how it is with you and me if you dare to speak before I'm done. I will go downstairs and jump in our car—the car I paid for—and you will never find me."

Bobbie remained quiet.

"My Daddy didn't want you comin' 'round anymore, but I told him I didn't care what he said; I was going to see you again. I stood by you. He took me out to the woodshed and gave me the beating of my life. When I told you what he did to me, you promised me you would never ever hit me, and I ran away with you. I left my Daddy and my sisters behind. But when you hit me last night, something snapped inside me like a broken banjo string. I think it was my heart breaking—breaking again, in the same place it broke before."

I don't know whether Bobbie said she was sorry or her face conveyed the same message, but Ashley gave a response as if she had.

"Sorry isn't going to cut it. I know you've been under a lot of pressure, and things haven't worked out the way you planned, but from here on out, we're going to do things my way, or I'm outta here."

The gag order must have been lifted because Bobbie whispered something.

Ashley responded, "I don't know if there is a you and me anymore, and I'm not gonna decide that until all this drug business is over and behind us."

Then she hollered down, "Cliff, can you come up here?"

I wasn't too nimble with my crutches on the stairway, but I made it up the skinny little steps using my left leg and dragging my crutches under my right arm.

When I entered the room, I could see the ire erupting in Bobbie's face, but one glance from Ashley and the fires of anger were extinguished, or at least smoldering under a cover.

"Now Cliff and I went to Captain Atkins to make the drug deal, but he balked and took off. So, I took Cliff to the hospital. They X-rayed his leg and fixed him up proper-like, but he never said a word about what happened here last week. I told you he wouldn't, and he didn't."

I wanted to speak up and tell Bobbie of my theory that if I made the drug deal, then I would be implicated and could never tell anyone, but Ashley was firmly in charge, and I didn't think anyone should speak unless she asked them to.

"Now, I'm gonna give you back your cell phone, and you're gonna call Eddie. Tell him you sent me and Cliff to make the deal last night, and Atkins balked because he didn't know us. Tell him it's okay. That me and Cliff are with you and we'll meet him again whenever he wants to finish the deal.

"What about me?"

"You're going to stay right here until this whole mess is over."

"No, Eddie will want to know why I can't go."

"Tell him you can't."

"Why not?"

"I don't care. Tell him you got business elsewhere. Tell him you have the plague. I don't care what you tell him as long as he sets up the deal for me and Cliff."

"But he'll want to know who Cliff is."

In the pregnant silence, I said, "Tell him I'm your investor, your money man." I had switched to academic role—trying to figure out how to solve a presented problem. I said, "Look, if you're going to tell a lie, you should tell it as close to the truth as possible. Why not tell Eddie that half your stash was stolen in P-Town, and I have a vested interest in your selling the other half? That much is true."

"What's your vested interest?"

"You know my interest. I don't want anything from you. I just want my freedom." What I really wanted, I didn't say. "That's where the lying part comes in. You tell him my interest is in the money. I was your backer for the money, and I want to be there to ensure I get my investment back. He can even check me out online. My picture and resume are on the college website. It's clear I'm not a cop."

Bobbie bought my being the financial backer and not wanting any money from her, but she still had doubt on her face. There was still the question of whether Ashley would go with me or Bobbie when everything was over. Neither Bobbie nor I knew that answer.

Bobbie didn't bring it up because she was afraid of what that answer might be. I certainly wasn't going to bring it up. That would infuriate Bobbie, and the timing wasn't right with Ashley. Besides, I still had time to convince her. We were going out on a drug deal together. What's that thing about becoming closer after being together in a foxhole?

"What do you think, Bobbie?" She seemed surprised I was even asking.

"I think Eddie has to meet you, and you have to convince him."

Ashley intervened. "You call Eddie. Now! See if you can get him over here this morning."

Bobbie glared at me. I don't know what she was thinking. Was she thinking Ashley was going to run off with me? I was thinking how fantastic that would be. Neither one of us knew what Ashley was thinking.

All that thinking ended when Ashley said, "Call him!" She gave Bobbie the phone. "And keep it on speaker."

Bobbie did as she was told, and Eddie answered.

"Bobbie, what the hell?"

"I know, I know. I screwed up."

"Atkins wanted no part of two strangers. Who was that guy anyway? Is he a cop?"

"No. No. Nothing like that. He's my financial backer."

"And why weren't you there?"

"I'm in Florida. I had to fly back."

"What? Why didn't you tell me?"

"I didn't have time. Some pretty bad people in Tampa lent me the money to buy the merchandise and I was overdue with the payment. They wanted me back there right away, or else!" She looked at Ashley as if to get approval for how she was handling Eddie.

She continued, "Cliff . . . Cliff Stone—that's his name."

She said it like it came with a dose of castor oil in her mouth.

"He advanced me the money and I flew down there."

"What was he doing at the boat?"

"Cliff insisted on going with Ashley to protect his investment." My name still sounded like something she should spit out.

"Who is this guy?"

"He's okay. He works at the college in Boston. I've done business with him in the past. He moves a lot of drugs." Bobbie nodded toward Ashley as if he was still seeking her approval.

Eddie said, "I don't get it."

"Look. I got into a little jam. I didn't tell you, but I lost half my stash in P-Town."

"What do you mean you lost it?"

"It was stolen."

"By who?"

"By some strangers that I met in Hyannis. They sucked me in. I was lucky they didn't kill me."

"You gotta be careful, Bobbie. Gotta know who you're dealing with. This a dangerous game. The Captain was too smart to deal with someone he didn't know."

"I know. Captain Atkins balked, but if you could explain things to him, they would bring the merchandise back and make the deal. Please, Eddie, I would consider it a personal favor."

Eddie was quiet for a short pause.

"My finder's fee the same?" he asked.

"A thousand," Bobbie answered.

"I think it should be fifteen hundred," Eddie said, "for all the trouble I gotta go through."

"Twelve-fifty, that's all I can afford. I'm coming out of this with nothing."

"Deal. I expect Captain Atkins back late this afternoon. I can talk to him. But first, I have to check out this Cliff guy."

"He and Ashley are at the house. Should I call them and tell them to expect you?"

"Yeah, I'll go right over."

Eddie showed up around nine o'clock. This time, he knew enough to park out back. Ashley met him at the back door, greeting him with a heavy dose of Southern charm.

"Eddie! Good to see you again. Sorry for the little mix-up the other night. Would you like some coffee?"

"Sure."

"Come on in. Take your coat off. Throw it over that chair."

They came into the kitchen, and I nodded hello.

"Eddie, this is Cliff Stone. He's the one who financed the deal. We had a little glitch when Bobbie got robbed, and Cliff saved our bacon."

I gave a phony smile that said I'm not doing it for humanitarian purposes. "I advanced Bobbie the money because she said the sale was all set up, and it was a sure thing. I came all the way down from Boston to make sure it went all right. Protect my investment."

"Yeah, Bobbie told me."

Eddie still seemed a little tentative, so I tried to put him at ease.

"I'm a college professor. Teach history. You can check me out on the university's website."

He looked down at my freshly-cast leg.

"The leg was a skiing accident up in New Hampshire a couple of weeks ago.

I laid it on thick. Told him the courses I was teaching, my kids' ages, and how I had to make money to pay for their college educations. I gave him details about my accident. I was on the Rattlesnake Trail at Wildcat Mountain. Conditions were icy, and there wasn't a sufficient base of snow. My ski caught a twig sticking up through the snow, and down I went—a non-displaced fracture of the tibia. I used my strategy of lying as close to the truth as possible.

Eddie said, "Atkins should be back late this afternoon. I'll talk to him. Get back to you."

I said, "We sure do appreciate it," and shook his hand.

Ashley snuggled up to his arm and said, "We sure do appreciate it." Ashley gave him her phone number, walked him to the door, and hugged him on his way out.

Ashley made turkey sandwiches for lunch. It was late afternoon when Eddie called back. Captain Atkins was back in port. He was going out again that night. The deal was set, same time, same place.

Ashley went upstairs to tell Bobbie. She warned her to remain quiet, and then she repeated the threat of never speaking to her again. I hobbled up to try to make peace.

"It's all set," I said. "It's all going to work out okay."

Bobbie glared at me. She had no intention of smoking a peace pipe.

Ashley was in no mood for more discussion. "I've been up all night. I'm going to lie down. Tonight, it all ends."

She went into the Ocean Room and closed the door behind her. Bobbie and I both heard the click of the lock. Since Bobbie was tied to the bed, the click was to inform me that my crutch was not welcomed in Ashley's bedroom. Bobbie seemed pleased.

"Can I get you another sandwich?"

Bobbie's glare followed me out of the Author's Room. The Ocean Room door was closed. My nap for the night ahead was in the lonely Captain's Room, where Penny and I no longer slept and where I never encountered Missy.

SHIPS IN THE NIGHT

The Captain was on the rear deck when we approached the Becky Sue. The motor was running, and Poke stood behind him. We greeted him, and he said, "Stop talking." It was a command like we were his crew. He expected compliance. He glanced all around the docks. "Come aboard."

He helped Ashley over the rail but gave a look that said I was too feeble.

"What's wrong with you?" he asked.

"Nothing. I'll be fine." I sat on the rail and swung my legs aboard, tightly gripping the duffel bag and my crutches.

He led us below into the galley. Ashley went right down. I hesitated, and Poke said, "I'll hold those." He took my crutches, and I hopped down the three stairs. My crutches didn't follow, but he did. The galley smelled like coffee, an herb shop, and a hint of fish slime, but it was as warm and toasty as the night air was cold and icy.

The Captain said, "Sit."

Ashley sat on the bench of a small kitchen table, and I hobbled over to a stool in the corner.

"Why don't you put that bag of yours down right over there where we can both keep an eye on it."

"I'll hold onto it if it's all the same to you."

"It's not. I'm responsible for the safety of all my passengers and crew. Put the bag down." He said it firmly as if there was an "or else" implied. He nodded like it had all been rehearsed. "Poke, check him out."

Poke came over to me and said, "Stand up."

I stood up, still clutching the bag.

"Put the bag down."

I set the bag down at my feet.

He said, "Arms up."

I raised my arms.

He kicked the bag away and then slid his big hands tight down my sides, repeating in increments around my upper body until he made sure I wasn't armed. His fingers weaved their way across my chest to make sure I wasn't wearing a wire. He made the same examination of my lower half, not showing the least bit of shame feeling all around my private parts.

"He's clean," he said to the Captain, and the Captain's eyes shifted to Ashley.

Poke looked over at Ashley with a salacious grin on his face. "Now you, little lady."

"Wait a minute," I said, we're just here to drop off—"

"I'm afraid I don't know who you are," Atkins said.

Ashley said, "Look, Bobbie and I are friends of Eddie." She said it matter-of-factly like she had been Eddie's friend for years. "My partner, Bobbie, couldn't make it, so she sent me instead. I brought him along for protection."

Atkins grinned at that.

It didn't ring true to me either, so I countered, "Business manager is more my role. Do you have the money?"

He raised his finger to his mouth in a shush gesture. "Check her, Poke."

Poke gave her the same going over as me except for the extra attention in the crevices around her breasts. Ashley looked at me. Did she want me to intervene? Did she want me to look away? Whatever she wanted didn't show. Her expression was fixed. Her eyes didn't blink. Her breath stopped. She was frozen while this Neanderthal groped her. If time stands still, nothing that's happening keeps on happening.

"She's clean, too."

The Captain said, "Good." Then he looked at Ashley and said, "Sorry about that, honey, but I'm a careful man."

He got up and grabbed a mug out of the cabinet. "You want some coffee? Poke just made it. He doesn't look like much, but he brews a good cup of coffee."

We both declined. He placed his mug under the spout of a café-sized urn, and black coffee steamed out.

"It's time to get out of here." He looked at Poke, "Cast off, Po-man."

I said, "Wait a minute. We're not going anywhere. We're here to do business."

"I only do business out there." He pointed toward the mouth of the harbor.

"How do we know you have the money?"

He nodded to Poke, who opened a burlap gunnysack filled with wads of money.

"Any objections?" Atkins opened his pea coat and exposed a gun in a holster.

I voiced no objection. Either Ashley didn't notice the gun, or she was taking charge again. With all her Southern charm, she said, "Captain, we're on a tight deadline. Couldn't we just do our business now and be gone?"

"I told you. I'm a careful man."

Poke headed for the stairs. The Captain said, "You two can make yourselves at home down here in the cuddy where it's warm. Tricky piloting out of this harbor." He followed Poke up the stairs and closed the hatch behind him.

Ashley looked at me and said, "What do you think?"

I said, "Did you see that gun?"

"Yeah. I grew up with guns. They don't scare me. What do you think about the deal?"

I think he's going to go out beyond the three-mile limit or something and make it out there. Maybe he'll do some fishing. I don't know. Then he'll return us to shore in the afternoon. Do you think Bobbie will be all right until then?"

"Yeah. I left her some food and a chamber pot if she needs it. She has her cell phone in case of an emergency."

"What? You left her a phone?" Suddenly, my stomach felt a little queasy. I don't think it was the motion of the boat in the water. "Aren't you worried she might call someone? Eddie. What about Eddie?"

"I told her I'll never speak to her again if she does anything like that. And I mean it. She knows I do."

Just then, Poke came back into the galley carrying a bunch of ship's rope. He said to Ashley, "Cap'n wants to speak to you for a minute."

Ashley got up, and I said I was going too.

Poke said, "No! Just the little lady."

Ashley looked at me and said, "I'll be all right," and she went up the stairs.

I was sitting up in the lower berth of a bunk with my legs outstretched on the mattress. Poke reached in and grabbed my hips, lifted them, and flipped me over on my belly. It happened so fast, and his grip was so strong that I felt like a rag doll with my head buried in a pillow. He pulled my arms back and tied them together like a rodeo cowboy hog-tying a steer.

"What the hell are you doing?

"Shuddup or you'll be talkin' outta a broken jaw."

He was working fast, tying the rope around my torso and my legs. I was lying in the bed like the Curse of the Mummy. I didn't say anything. When he was sure I was secure, he went back up the stairs. Secure? The ropes were so tight that they cut into my sides whenever I moved. Even the new cast on my leg was crumbling under the pressure of the ropes. On his way out, he shut the galley lights.

Here I was again like I started—a prisoner in the dark. Penny and the kids had no idea where I was. There was no Missy on board to save me. What happened to Ashley?

Smite thine enemies seemed like such good advice now. *Missy, if you can hear me now, kill them all. Call to your husband and his crew from the deep. Save us. Save me.*

The engine noise increased markedly as Captain Atkins pushed the throttle forward. The galley heaved up and down in a rocking motion. We were out of the harbor into open waters. I rolled toward the wall to steady myself so I wouldn't fall out of the bunk.

After a while, Poke opened the hatch, flipped on the lights, and came back down the stairs. "Coffee'll warm you up," he said. He wasn't talking to me.

Ashley was behind him. "It's colder than a you-know-who's you-know-what," she said, and Poke laughed. She barely glanced over at me. Instead, she headed to the coffee urn and poured herself a cup. She cupped the warm mug in her hands and said, "Boy, this feels good. Can I pour you one, Mr. Poke?" All that groping had been forgiven.

"Yes, Ma'am." No telling what he expected next.

"I said, "Ashley, what's going on?"

Poke said, "Shut up!" and he started over toward me.

"No, that's okay," Ashley said. "I'll tell you what's going on. I left Bobbie a phone after you cuffed her to the bed. She called Eddie, and Eddie called the Captain. There's pretty good cell phone coverage all the way out to Monomoy Island. They now know about you. You've been outsmarted."

I couldn't believe what I was hearing. She was almost happy about it. Another betrayal. I gave up. I was done with women. Forever. The only problem was that forever might just be until we got out to wherever we were heading. Deep water, no doubt. Icy cold. I'd be dead in minutes. One last time, I remembered the Dostoevsky quote, *Only to live, to live and live! Life, whatever it may be!* I wanted to be home with Penny and the kids.

Ashley looked over to Poke. "Go grab the Captain's cup, and I'll warm it up for him."

Poke bounded up the stairs, and Ashley reached into the duffel bag of drugs."

I said, "Ashley—"

"Quiet!" Her whisper carried the authority of an Army general.

Poke came back down the stairs with the Captain's mug and gave it to Ashley.

She said, "You better check his ropes."

He came over and grabbed a hunk of rope in each of his powerful hands. Then he lifted me off the bed and shook me as if some part of my anatomy was going to shake loose. Nothing did, and he dropped me back on the bed.

"Here's your coffee."

He thanked her as if they were bosom buddies from the old days.

She said, "You better stay down here and watch him. I'll bring the Captain his coffee." With that, she brought the Captain's mug up the stairs. She left the hatch open and called the Captain in the wheelhouse in her sweetest voice, "I got something to warm you up."

She quickly came back down and again warmed herself on her mug of hot coffee. She addressed Poke. "I give you a lot of credit. It takes a bunch to face that cold, and you actually fish out there?"

Poke said, "Yeah, you never quite get used to it, but you just have to tough it out." He made a fist and flexed his arm like a bodybuilder.

"Here's to you and all the fishermen who brave the cold for us civilians." She raised her cup in a toast, and they both drank some coffee.

"Tell me more," she said.

Poke sidled up next to her and clicked cups. She looked into his eyes over the top of her mug as they drank. "What d'ya wanna know?" he said.

All that flirtation. Who was this girl? The daughter her father and sisters rejected, the docile partner of Bobbie The Terrible, the nurse who cared for me, cuddled up next to me like a loving woman? That's it. She's a woman. There's no more to say. You never know what's going on inside a woman's pretty little head. What did Oscar Wilde say? Something like *her face is a work of fiction.*

The Captain hollered down, "Poke, get up here!"

Poke took a last gulp of coffee and said, "I gotta go." He took one giant step up two stairs and stuck his head out. "What's up, Captain?"

"Get out here. I thought I saw something coming our way."

Poke jumped out and left the hatch open.

Ashley put her cup down and searched the utensil drawer. She took out a small steak knife and came at me.

"Ashley, no! What are you going to do?"

"Quiet!" She said in a whisper. "I emptied half a vial of LSD into their coffees. It won't be long now."

"But what are we going to do?"

"I don't know. Haven't figured that yet. All I know is they will both turn into mushes any minute." She started sawing through the ropes around my legs. Then she rolled me over and cut the lines around my hands. His sailor knots wouldn't lend themselves to unravel easily. I would have been helpless in the water.

She rolled me back and started sawing through the ropes around my arms when the boat turned hard to the right, and the Captain gunned the engine. Ashley fell over on top of me, and the knife jabbed into my shoulder just below my clavicle.

"Ow. Not again."

We were lying together in the bunk. "I'm sorry." She used the blood-tipped knife to finish cutting the rope that set me free. "Press on the wound."

A loud thump stopped the boat dead. Ashley and I were hurled forward into the wall of the bunk. It felt like the boat was somersaulting in the water. Then it halted and fell back, tumbling us out of the bunk onto the floor, which was now drastically tilting.

A loud cracking sound came from below, followed by the sound of water rushing in. The motor sputtered and stopped. Everything went quiet except for the flow of water.

The galley was now like Slanty Sam's Shanty in an amusement park—laying on its side slightly tipped forward. I gave Ashley a boost to get her standing, and she gave me a hand to pull me up. She cautiously headed up the stairs and peeked out of the hatch. She stepped onto the deck and called back to me, "No one's here."

The water from below was beginning to seep into the galley. I grabbed the gunny sack of money. I wasn't sure what I was going to do with it. I couldn't buy a ticket out of there. I managed to leave the galley and found my crutches on the deck. They were still no match for Poke's hook.

Ashley had made her way to the wheelhouse. "The Captain is lying on the floor. He's unconscious."

"Where's Poke?"

"I don't know. Don't see him."

I looked around hard. Poke was not aboard. The boat had run aground on one of those shifting shoals off Monomoy Island. It listed heavily to one side.

"Get the captain's gun. Can you see Poke in the water?"

"No. I can't see anything out there."

The sky and the ocean surrounded us in a black canopy with holes where starlight punched through, and the only sounds in the night were the lapping of waves against the side of the boat. If Poke was in the water, he couldn't call for help.

In the distance, the moon peeked out from behind a drifting cloud, and soon, the full moon provided a spotlight all around us. Still, there was no sign of Poke, so I threw a life-saving ring into the water anyway.

Ashley came down the wheelhouse stairs, balancing the gun on the palm of her hand like a waiter carrying a tray of dishes, and she hurled it into the ocean.

She grabbed my arm and looked about at the vastness that surrounded us.

"Now, what do we do?"

I wasn't sure, but I would have rather had the gun to do it with. I wrapped my arm around her.

"Maybe stepping into the water and onto the shoal we hit will lead to the island.

The air was still but cold. I inched toward the rail and tested the water with my fingers. It felt like dry ice, and my hand burned from the cold. Stepping into that water was a stupid idea.

"I don't know what to do."

Ashley shrieked, "Oh my God, Cliff!"

I turned around, and the Captain came out of the wheelhouse and faced us. A trickle of dried blood ran down his forehead, and his face had an odd look. He asked us, "Did you see it?"

"See what?"

He turned and pointed into the darkness. "The three-masted schooner—a ship—heading right for us. It was magnificent, magnificent, magnificent." He kept repeating *magnificent* as he walked like Rubberman past us toward the side of the boat.

Ashley grabbed his hand and coaxed him back up to the wheelhouse. I followed with my crutches, ready if he turned on her, but he didn't. She sat him back in his seat.

"Sit. Stay." It sounded like she was talking to a dog. "Steer the boat."

He ran his hand around the steering wheel. "It's round, like the Earth is round, and Davy Jones is six fathoms down."

Just then, we heard a motor in the distance. A small boat approached us from the rear of the Betty Sue, its outboard motor wake shining in the moonlight.

"We're saved," I said.

A voice rang out from the boat, "Ashley!"

It was Bobbie.

BREAKING NEWS

US COAST GUARD PRESS RELEASE

COAST GUARD RESCUES ONE SEAMAN OFF MONOMOY ISLAND.

At 2:00 AM yesterday, the Coast Guard cutter, AA Huxley, out of Chatham, Massachusetts, conducted a rescue of the fishing boat, Betty Sue, that had wrecked on the shoals of Monomoy Island. The only person aboard was a local fisherman, Captain Cecil Atkins of Harwich Port, who was delirious at the time of rescue. He was rushed to Cape Cod Hospital, where he remains in good condition. Later today, the body of his crewman, Stanley Pokowski, was recovered from the waters near Monomoy. A satchel filled with Fentanyl pills and LSD vials with a street value of a quarter million dollars was found aboard the Betty Sue.

– Captain Everett Sommerfeld, USCG Station, Chatham, Massachusetts

TWO YEARS LATER

FISHERMAN RELEASED

CHATHAM FISHERMAN RELEASED FROM PRISON

BY TOM STEELE

A well-known sea captain, Cecil Atkins, was released from MCI-Concord today, where he had served two years on charges of possession of drugs with intent to distribute. Captain Atkins maintains his innocence and has stuck to his story that he did not know about the drugs onboard the Betty Sue the night it ran aground on the shoals of Monomoy Island. His story is the same today as the day he went to jail. "We were on our way to go skate fishing south from out of Stage Harbor when, about 20 miles out, we were nearly rammed by a rogue schooner bearing down on us. I had to turn hard starboard and gun it to avoid being cut in two. That's when I ran aground, and Pokowski went overboard. I have no idea where the drugs came from."

A black pickup truck hauling a cube trailer with the side painted Seaside Landscaping pulled up to a house in St. Petersburg, Florida. A young man hopped out of the passenger side and opened the back of the trailer. He came riding down the ramp of the trailer on a lawnmower. The pickup truck driver got out and grabbed an edge trimmer from the back of the trailer. She was a husky woman in denim coveralls.

Her cell phone rang, and she answered, "Seaside, Bobbie here." She continued, "Yes, Sweetie, I remember. We have one more job to finish, and then I'll be home. Love you. Bye."

The commencement ceremony for the University of California San Francisco graduate degree in Nursing occurred on the south campus's lawn. After what seemed like interminable speeches in the hot California sun and a long parade of graduates picking up their degrees, caps flew into the air. The afternoon was filled with family dinners, cookouts, and parties all over campus.

Around 8:00 PM that evening, a couple walked hand-in-hand onto the beach to watch the sun set into the grand Pacific.

"My God, you did it. You're a Nurse Practitioner."

The graduate beamed with pride. When the sun fell below the ocean horizon, the sky turned saffron orange, and pride turned to tenderness. She leaned over and planted a kiss on her partner's cheek.

"I couldn't have done it without your help, Alex.

"Don't be silly. You've been a star since you first came to work at the hospital."

"And now we'll be working together."

Alex took her hand. "I love you."

"I love you, too."

Lake Winnipesaukee sparkled with sunlight. A fourteen-year-old girl skimmed along on waterskis behind a Boston Whaler with a 35 horsepower outboard driven by a middle-aged-plus man in a bathing suit. Her younger brother acted as spotter to signal in case she took a fall.

When she did, the boy yelled out, "She fell. She fell. My turn, Dad."

The man brought the boat around to pick up his daughter. His hair was thinning and gray. He had a scar on his right shoulder and his right thigh. He told his kids he got them from sharp tree branches that cut him when he broke his leg skiing.

An elderly couple sat in the front parlor of a Mansard Victorian facing the ocean in Chatham. He was a retired social worker from New Jersey, and his wife had for many years dabbled in the occult. In her previous life, she was known for her Tarot card readings.

"I'm disappointed, Henry."

"What about dear?"

"I was certain this house had a spirit present when we bought it, but I can find no trace of her anywhere."

"Maybe it's true."

"What's true?"

"Like it said in the book we picked up at the Yellow Umbrella Book Store, Missy's spirit remained in the house waiting a hundred fifty years for her husband to return from the sea, and one cold December night, his ghost ship sailed into the harbor. If you like, I will take you back to the Seaside Cemetery, and you can commune with them there."

Oh, Henry. You've been reading too many ghost stories.

THE END

THE TRUE HISTORY OF THE HOUSE ON MAIN STREET

1

Author's Note

This *Afterword* is the true history of *The House on Main Street*. When I first walked into the magnificent structure, like the character Cliff Stone in this fictional tale, "I felt as much an affinity for the bones of that house as my flesh did for my own skeleton." I also felt a spooky presence that prompted the made-up story of Cliff, Bobbie, Ashley, and the ghost Mercie.

Cliff said of his students, "They have no sense of history. To them, the assassinations of Julius Caesar, Abraham Lincoln, and JFK are all contemporaneous events from ancient times." Who among us hasn't had trouble remembering dates from the history we learned in school?

By contrast, we remember our own histories through our human experience—where we were and who we were with at the time. The richer the human experience, the more vivid the memory, and the more unforgettable the history.

Rather than tell the house's history as a set of meaning-less names, dates, and places—metadata in today's lexicon—I will tell it in terms of the stories of the people who lived there. Only when the ghosts of the past come alive in stories do we glimpse into true history.

I want to emphasize that although *The House* spawned the fictional tale, the people who lived there in those times bear no valid relationship to the made-up characters. The story is entirely fabricated.

Long before the house was built, the land belonged to the Monomoit Tribe, whose village stood about where the house rests today. How the land was transferred from the Monomoits to the settlers from Europe is a big part of the history, even though the initial transaction occurred almost 200 years before the house was built.

When the house was built around 1875, a small sapling, no more than a twig, was growing in the backyard. It took 150 years for that sapling to grow into a giant Norwegian Pine that hovered over the back of the house like a giant sentinel.

The original owners of the house, Captain Everett and Mrs. Mercie Hammond Patterson, lived there for about the first 50 of those 150 years, and the five families who owned it after spanned about another 100. That brings us to the present day. The house still stands tall on its red brick foundation and has weathered all those years against the rain, snow, ocean gales, and even the occasional hurricane winds. Like the ghost, Mercie, she is a strong lady.

In 2019, a large horizontal bough from the Norwegian pine came crashing down on the rear deck in a storm. For many years, it held a rope swing that delighted generations of children and adults returning to their childhoods. A skilled arborist reluctantly declared that the rest of the tree had to be taken down before it landed on the house. When the tree was felled, the sawed-off trunk measured two-and-a-half feet across and exposed hundreds of tree rings.

I like to run my hand along those tree rings and contemplate the lives of the families who lived under the shade of that tree. In each ring of the tree, an entire year of a family's joys and sorrows took place. It is difficult to count all the rings of the tree, just as it would be difficult to recount all that happened to those people, but to acknowledge their presence is to honor their existence on the good earth where the house still stands.

To understand the true history of *The House*, we shall delve into the histories of the Monomoit Tribe, which first lived on the land, the European settlers who traded with them, and, to a limited extent, the six families who occupied the house after it was built.

Think of the length of time over which this history took place this way. Let's say that your good fortune allows you to live 100 years—a centennial life span. Think of all you could cram into those years. (Not enough, I know.)

When the Pilgrims landed on Plymouth Rock in 1620, the indigenous peoples had already been in Chatham and its surrounding lands for hundreds of those centennial life spans.

This *Afterword* focuses on the roughly four-and-a-half centennial lifetimes from when the first explorers arrived on the land to when the house was built to the 150 years later when Cliff Stone's story was told. Unlike Cliff's story, this *Afterword* is the true story of *The House* and those who haunt it still.

2

It All Started with Trouble in Europe

To understand how a European-style Italianate Victorian house came to be built on these native lands, we must go back to sixteenth-century Europe, where much of the trouble began. The European and Asian continents had a rich history of religious strife. Stories of inquisitions, expulsions, and the searches for heretics and infidels abound. Where repentance and conversion didn't work, burning at the stake or beheading were the preferred remedies.

After the fall of the Roman Empire, much of Europe was Catholic. The tale is told that in 1517, Martin Luther nailed ninety-five theses to the door of the cathedral at Wittenberg, Germany, to start the Protestant Reformation. It is more likely that he tacked them up—like on a bulletin board—to garner support to reform what many saw as faults in the Catholic church. But to picture this revolutionary with a large hammer and a blacksmith-hewn nail banging on the cathedral door is a more fitting beginning to what was to become a bloodbath of religious zeal that spread across Europe.

It started with disagreements over buying Indulgences—forgiveness from sin—from members of the clergy. To some, this was not a holy act. When their "protesting" was unsuccessful in reforming the church, these "protestants"—who at that point still considered themselves Catholic—started breaking away from the church.

The buying of indulgences was sort of like today's carbon credits. "If I pay to pollute the world (with my sins), I can jet away with a clear conscience."

As a result of their zeal, the protestants engendered prejudice, excommunication, and, finally, persecution. Only then did the Protestant Reformation become a serious movement separate from the Catholic church.

Around the same time in England (1534), King Henry VIII was looking for a solution to his "great matter," which was to produce a male heir. He stumbled on the idea of dumping the 40-year-old queen, Catherine of Aragon, in favor of the 25-year-old beauty, Ann Boleyn.

Pope Clement VII didn't like that idea. With the Protestant Reformation in full gear, Henry jumped ship and made himself the Supreme Head of the (Protestant) Church of England. In his religious zeal, he also bedded the young Boleyn girl and made her queen.

The European Catholics and Protestants spent years killing one another in the name of God and country. The bodies were piling up. On St Bartholomew's Day, in 1572, French Catholics murdered a bunch of French Protestants. The battles raged on for hundreds of years.

Lest you think Europe was not ecumenical, there were also many inquisitions and expulsions of heretic Jews and Muslim infidels by European monarchies. To add fuel to the fire of religious zeal, dissident Protestant groups even broke away from the Church of England.

Amid this turmoil in 1607, a bunch of English Separatists went to Leyden in the Netherlands to escape religious persecution. Over the years, they had trouble assimilating into Dutch culture. Can't blame them. Who'd want to wear those frilly collars?

In 1620, they and their followers joined a London stock company and set sail on the Mayflower for the New World colony of Virginia. Rough seas and storms forced them off their Virginia course to Plymouth on the coast of Cape Cod, where they established their new colony. This small band of God-fearing people seeking freedom from religious persecution and tyranny were full of hope for a new life in the New World.

Of course, it wasn't a new world. For centuries, it was the world inhabited by indigenous peoples, and although they never heard Martin Luther's hammer banging on the door of the Wittenberg Cathedral, the fallout from subsequent events in Europe would change their world forever.

3

Keepers of the Chatham Lands

For centuries before the settlers came, the people of the Wampanoag Nation lived all over Cape Cod. One of the tribes inhabited Monomoy—what is now called Chatham.

Unlike in Europe's patriarchal society, the traditions of the Wampanoags were more matriarchal. The women of the tribe appointed the sachem or chief, land was passed down from mother to daughter, and newlyweds moved in with the bride's family.

The women delegated two essential tasks to the men: trade with other Wampanoag tribes and, when a skirmish broke out, war.

The men fished and hunted all around Monomoy, while the women planted and harvested the "three sister" crops of corn, beans, and squash within the village. Families lived in round huts made of thatch and grass (called Wigwams), and they stored their harvested corn for the winter in grass sacks buried in the sandy dunes by the shore.

The Monomoits had likely seen white men as far back as the Middle Ages. The Norsemen from Iceland told tales of long strips of sandy bars they called *Furdustrandir* (Wonder Strands). These tales described the same beaches that lie between Nauset (at the Eastham-Orleans line) and Monomoy (Chatham).

Norsemen weren't the only white men they saw. In the 1500s, many European explorers and adventurers who had heard the tales that Columbus told of the New World sailed the waters around Cape Cod. The name America was designated on a 1502 map to honor an Italian explorer, Americo Vespucci, who wrote extensively about his adventures in the New World.

Cape Cod was named by the British Explorer Bartholomew Gosnold, who came in 1602.

4

The Land on which The House Was Built

One particular explorer of interest to the history of *The House* is the French explorer Samuel de Champlain. In Dec 1606, fourteen years before the Pilgrims arrived in Plymouth, he sailed down from Port Royal, the French Colony in Nova Scotia, in his three-masted, square-sail ship. The sand bars and shifting tides made for treacherous waters, and their ship ended up with a broken rudder. They anchored outside Stage Harbor, where Cliff and Ashley (in our story) went to make their drug deal.

Forgive me if I refer to the fictional characters from the novel. After living with them in my mind for several years, they seem real to me, and I hope you will feel the same way after reading about them. Thus, I will use them to shed light on the history of *The House*.

Champlain reported observing five or six hundred inhabitants when he first arrived. The Monomoits were not that large in number, so neighboring tribes likely showed up to see the white men. A similar phenomenon takes place today. The population of Chatham swells with people from all over who come to watch spectacles, such as the Fourth of July Parade and the arrival of the fishing boats at the Chatham Pier.

Champlain drew a map of the area, which he called Port Fortuné. His map from 1606 of the coastline and the Monomoit Village is shown below in Figure 1. I have overlaid it with several current landmarks: Stage Harbor, Chatham Harbor, Mill Pond, the Holway Street Beach, North Beach, and Ryder's Cove.

Eventually, the explorers lowered their small boat from the deck and rowed ashore to repair their ship's broken rudder. They landed on the beach between what is now Andrew Harding Lane and Holway Street, reporting that the natives were friendly and helpful.

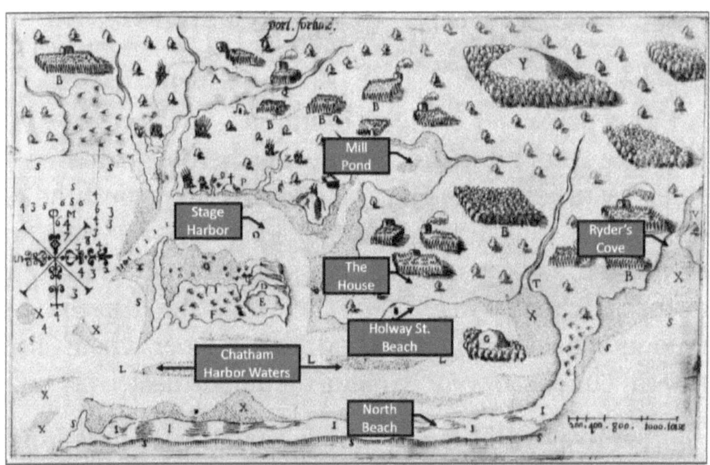

Fig.1 Champlain's map of Chatham and the Monomoit Village overlaid with current landmarks. Courtesy of Chatham Historical Society.

The House now stands where de Champlain observed the Monomoit Village. If you walk from the house across Main Street and walk a couple of hundred yards down Holway Street to the stone revetment at the shoreline, you will be standing where there was once a beach—the one on which Champlain landed and the one that had the sandy dunes in which the natives stored their corn.

On New Year's Eve of 1987, a storm caused a breakthrough in North Beach's outer bank, and the Holway Street beach began to erode. On Halloween of 1991, the wrath of Mother Nature created the "Perfect Storm" (of movie fame), which caused additional erosion and the loss of nine shorefront houses. The revetment was added in 1996.

Cliff Stone, being a history buff, knew about the houses that had disappeared into the sea. When he walked in his drug-induced state from the beach at the end of Holway Street to *The House*, he entered some kind of time warp in which the last remaining Wigwam and *The House* both existed at the same time.

At first, the French traded axes, telescopes, and utensils with the natives for furs, food, and navigation help, but trouble was soon to brew. The French were ever suspicious of the "savages" and eventually saw them as thieves who would take what they wanted without paying. Whether that's true or the native culture didn't recognize "ownership" in the same way the French did is lost to posterity. What is certain is in several skirmishes, some sailors and some natives were killed.

5

The Great Dying

The trouble the Monomoits had with the French was not unique to Monomoy. All over the east coast of America, there was an uneasy peace between European settlers, adventurers, or traders and these Native Americans. Death came to both sides whenever the peace was broken. Of course, some Europeans died in the harsh winter environment, while the natives saved many of them.

The biggest death came from an unexpected source.

Once the Native Americans and the Europeans started interacting, a deadly plague beset the natives. Between 1616 and 1619, nearly 90 percent of them were wiped out. It is likely that European diseases carried by rats on ships and transmitted into the fresh waters of the land were such that the Native Americans' lack of natural immunity and habits of lifestyle (e.g., drinking from the streams and bathing in the fresh waters), caused them to be susceptible to the diseases when the Europeans were not.

This became known as "the great dying" and resulted in Cape Cod lands being even more sparsely populated than they had already been. The abundance of land and low number of natives made an attractive incentive for additional settlers to come. If word of mouth wasn't enough, the royal decree of King James I did the trick:

> *"Within these late years, there hath, by God's visitation, reigned a wonderful plague, the utter destruction, devastation, and depopulation of that whole territory, so as there is not left any that do claim or challenge any kind of interest therein," decreed the 1620 Charter of New England by King James I.*

Most of the deaths were north of Cape Cod in the Massachusetts Bay Colony and up to Nova Scotia, where there had been considerable interaction between Europeans and Native Americans. The plague did not reach as far south as Monomoy because the treacherous waters around Chatham prevented the Monomoits from interacting with many Europeans. However, the Monomoits were not immune to the swelling number of settlers who came to Plymouth Colony seeking land.

No proper name existed for the whole group of Indigenous peoples living In the Americas before the settlers came. They referred to themselves as diverse groups belonging to nations like the Wampanoag and tribes like the Monomoit. When I referred to the entire group above, I called them by the common term history has given them—Native Americans, which incorporates the prejudice that their land was "American" even before the Europeans arrived and named it.

The other common term used to describe this larger population is "Indian." That term came about because Columbus set sail for the East Indies. When he landed around the Bahamas, he called the natives that he encountered "Indians."

The term Indian became so pervasive that some of my friends who descended from indigenous peoples and who call themselves Native Americans also call themselves Indians. Their great-grandfathers must be turning over in their graves.

When referring to the collective group of indigenous peoples by a proper name, I will use the common-usage terms Native American and Indian—with great humility and respect.

6

The Settlers Who Bought the Land from the Indians

If you follow Main Street away from the lighthouse and head up the hill along Shore Road, you will encounter a fork in the road when you get to Ryder's Cove. The left fork becomes Old Comers Road. The story behind that name relates to the land on which *The House* is built.

When the Pilgrims were in exile in Leyden, they found merchants who would fund their journey to the New World in return for future payments. The agreement of 1620 was that these Pilgrims would hold in trust any stock or profits earned in the New World for seven years, after which they would split all gains with the merchants and divvy up what was left among themselves.

The colonists who signed that agreement came over on the *Mayflower* in 1620, the *Fortune* a year later, and the *Anne* three years later. When they formed the Plymouth Colony, they expected that they would share in one-half of the colony's riches at the end of the seven years.

The Pilgrims who founded Plymouth Colony were godly people. They had no intention of taking the land by force from the indigenous peoples of the Cape. In fact, the Plymouth Colony set up strict rules governing the purchase of land from the Indians.

The agreement was that wherever they found Indians who inhabited particular lands, the Indians had claim to those areas. The settlers could legally purchase the land from the Indians, but only with the approval of the Plymouth Colony authorities.

When there were few settlers and much land, the sachems or chiefs were happy to grant land privileges to a settler in need. The settlers would trade tools like axes and hammers for the land. In their English, common-law minds, the settlers were buying the land, while the Indians believed they were caretakers of the land and had a limited concept of ownership.

During those first seven years, when the Pilgrims had an agreement with the European merchants, additional settlers joined the Colony. The newcomers did not share in the promise of half the land's riches afforded the oldcomers.

Unfortunately, when the end of seven years came around, there wasn't enough money for the oldcomers to pay off the debts to the merchants. They raised money by selling some of their land to the newcomers in the Colony. Sometimes, the newcomers also desired to buy unclaimed land directly from the Indians—with the approval of the Plymouth Colony officials.

Until 1630, the Indians had sole control of the lands around Monomoy. But that year, the (Governor) Bradford Patent declared that all of Cape Cod became part of the Plymouth Colony. That encouraged additional settlements outside the bounds of Plymouth. Within about nine years, both Barnstable and Yarmouth were established.

The oldcomers felt that by virtue of their sacrifices in establishing the Colony, they had privileges in selecting which land they would get. The newcomers didn't agree, and arguments ensued. It wasn't until 1640 that another agreement was reached.

Governor Bradford set aside three large tracts of land for the oldcomers. The first encompassed Manomoit (now Chatham), South Orleans, Harwich, and Brewster—home to the Manomoits and Sauquatucketts. The other two were to the west—one around New Bedford and the other Narragansett Bay in what is now Rhode Island. The Monomoit (Chatham) Reserve is shown in Figure 2 below.

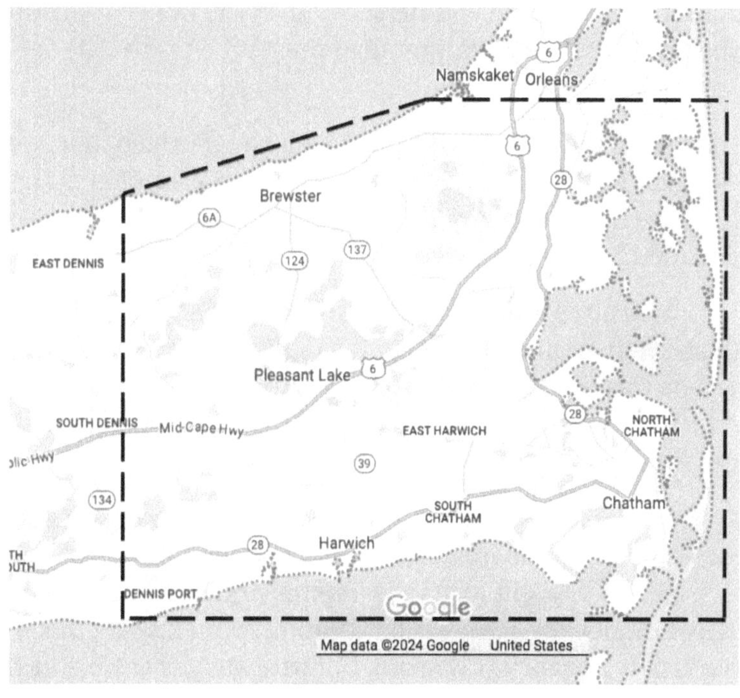

Fig.2 Governor Bradford's 1640 Reserve for "Old Comers."

For nearly twenty years, settlements flourished in Yarmouth and Eastham on both sides of the reserve that included Chatham, but no oldcomers had purchased any of the land from the Indians. That was about to change—in a way that caused even more trouble.

7

Nickerson Arrives in Chatham

In 1640, the year Governor Bradford set aside the Monomoit Reserve for oldcomers, William Nickerson was a 37-year-old Yarmouth resident with a wife and several kids. He had been a weaver in Norfolk County, England, where he was somewhat of a non-conformist and was persecuted by the holier-than-thou bishop of Norfolk. He emigrated to the New World at the age of 34. He was not an oldcomer.

He and his wife, who eventually had fourteen kids, were looking for land to raise their family. They were also looking ahead to a future in which they had enough land to divvy up for their kids to settle when they were grown.

With lively trade taking place between Yarmouth and Eastham, Nickerson must have scouted the Indian land in between. The land was fertile, extensive, unsettled, and sparsely populated by the friendly Monomoits. It seemed like an ideal place for his large family.

In 1656, he traded the sachem of Monomoit, a two-masted boat, twelve axes, hoes, and knives, six kettles, ten heavy wool coats, a hat, forty shillings in wampum, and twelve shillings in English money for a large tract of land encompassing much of what is now known as Chatham. Unfortunately, this violated the Bradford agreement that gave Monomoit preference to oldcomers.

Nickerson claimed no knowledge of that agreement, and in his mind, the fact that it had not been exercised in 16 years made it a moot point.

The Plymouth County authorities did not agree. In 1657, they dragged him into court and invalidated his purchase from the Monomoits because of the agreement with the oldcomers and because he hadn't gotten Plymouth County approval.

William Nickerson argued that he did not intend to break the law and was simply ignorant of the restrictions. He put himself at the mercy of the Court.

The Court was not sympathetic. He then petitioned them to allow the deal to proceed with whatever adjustment they deemed appropriate. They agreed that he might have a small portion of his purchased land.

He was unhappy with that judgment, and in 1659, he applied to recover the entire tract of land he had originally purchased from the Indians. They then ruled he might have the land if he paid a fine of 5 pounds per acre. He considered this tantamount to their approval of his purchase and took advantage of the fact that the court made no immediate attempt to collect the fines.

Sometime after 1659, his family began a settlement at Monomoit. In 1661, he even deeded 40 acres of his property to his daughter and her husband. That deed prompted the Marshall to come by and collect 200 pounds worth of goods or chattels—40 acres times 5 pounds per acre!

The Marshall found no assets worth 200 pounds. The court then put the entire Nickerson land up for sale. If he were lucky, they would give a small portion back to him and his family. That did not sit well with Nickerson, who considered himself the rightful owner.

In 1666, Nickerson went over the heads of the Plymouth Court to the King's representative. Remember, Plymouth Colony was still under the Crown in the 1600's. He sued for his entire original purchase.

He and his sons also wrote a scathing letter to the Court reproaching them for the unfair treatment they had given him. That got them imprisoned for several days until the King's representative interceded. For several years, lawsuits followed, some land was sold, and the controversy roared on.

It wasn't until 1672, sixteen years after Nickerson's original purchase, that he paid ninety pounds to the Court and secured a deed they deemed legal. The purchase was made from Mattaquason and his son Towsowet, the Monomoit sachems.

It's interesting to note how, by this time, the weight of English culture influenced the Manomoits—Towsowet's name as the son of "Matta-Quason" was recorded as John Quason on the deed. In fact, the family name Quason was still in the area's street directories into the 1900s, and a Quason Lane exists off Main Street in Harwich Port, less than ten miles from *The House.*

Nickerson's purchase included a large swath of land stretching from Ryder's Cove in the north, across Oyster Pond and Mill Pond, to Ridgevale and Hardings Beaches in the south. A map of Nickerson's first purchase is shown below in Figure 3, along with an insert of a current Google map of Chatham. The land where the house now stands (roughly equivalent to what is currently called the Old Village) was initially retained by the Monomoits but later purchased by Nickerson.

A plaque at the Nickerson Family Association on Orleans Road in Chatham provides a brief history of the Monomoits and Wapanaugs.

Thus, over 50 years after the Pilgrims landed in Plymouth, the bulk of Chatham land transferred from the Monomoits to the Nickersons. In much the same way, the bulk of the lands up and down the New England coast transferred from the Indians to the settlers.

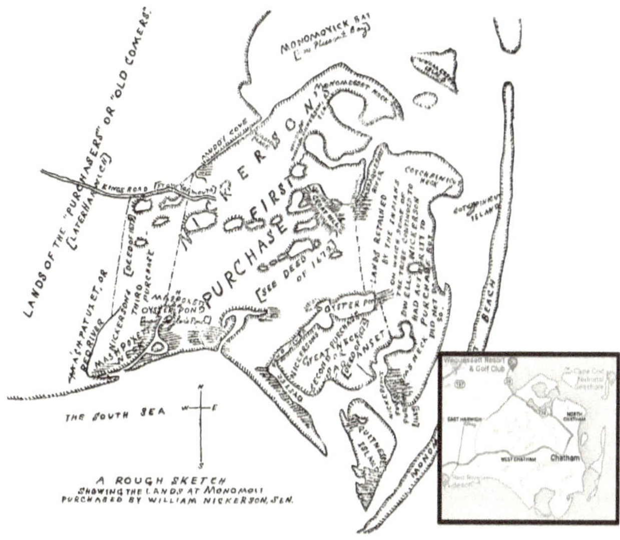

Fig.3 Nickerson's First Purchase with Chatham map insert. Courtesy of Chatham Historical Society and Google Maps

8

My Arrival

On a cold Spring Sunday in 1996, Anne and I drove up Main Street toward the lighthouse when a *For Sale* sign caught my eye. It was on the front lawn of *The House,* somewhat hidden by the hedge, as if the owner wasn't convinced it was to be sold.

I circled back.

The aluminum siding needed repair. A carpet of ivy snaked across the lawn and reached up to grab the siding with its gnarly fingers. The gothic design of the Mansard Victorian stood proud, and its G-Clef-like corbels with hanging dewdrops beckoned me—even if the weathered corbels and missing dewdrops gave the impression of a toothless smile.

I phoned the real estate agent and arranged to see it.

The many features described in the story—the high, tin ceiling in the dining room, the horsehair plaster walls covered with flowered wallpaper, the old monster furnace in the basement, the giant radiators on the first floor with their companion open grates in the ceiling, and the hidden ladder into the attic—all captured my fancy, and my heart.

The interior bones of the house oozed with the stuff of a bygone era.

In those days, I worked in engineering, where everything I did was analyzed, quantified, checked, and checked again. When we finished the house tour, we went to Christine's restaurant around the corner on Main Street. I put ketchup on my fries and made an offer to purchase, with no more foresight or surety than my ability to pay for lunch.

The woman who owned the house was an artist, which was clear from her furnishings and décor. I later purchased much of the furniture from her. She had lived in the house for 29 years. Her kids were grown and gone, and she was looking ahead to the future. I was enthralled with the past.

We transferred ownership just before Labor Day Weekend, and my extended family showed up to wish us well and see what I had been bragging about all summer. We also had one uninvited guest: Hurricane Edouard made landfall in Chatham that same weekend. Many of my family members joined Cape Cod residents and visitors escaping Edouard's potential destruction in a four-hour traffic jam at the narrow Sagamore Bridge.

The house that had stood vigil over the Atlantic for almost 150 years survived the storm's hurricane-force winds just fine. It groaned and creaked with each new gust of wind as if its ghosts were clinging to their haunt.

9

I Had to Know More

Over the next few months, my tree-hugging friends convinced me the house was indeed haunted. They identified the ghostly presence as strongest in the bedroom at the top of the back stairs leading up from the kitchen. I agreed.

The little kids who visited took turns scaring one another by looking into the room's deep, dark closet. I may have helped that along with ghost stories and by outfitting the closet's dress form in a blue silk cape and white mask that I brought home from Mardi Gras in Venice.

Still, I had to know more. At the Barnstable Registry of Deeds, I tracked the ownership back to the earliest records from the 1800's. What a joy to behold those giant registry books the size of butcher block countertops that recorded the legal chronology of generations of Cape Codders.

The documents themselves were works of art. Preprinted gothic letters said things like, "Know All Men by these Presents that . . ." The rest of each document was handwritten in 18th and 19th-century cursive, sometimes with the swirl of perfect penmanship, sometimes with the scribble of common-man script. Many of the principles described themselves as yeomen— a class of Englishman intermediate between the gentry and laborers.

The original document that conveyed the land from Horace Simmons to Captain Everett Patterson is shown below in Figure 4.

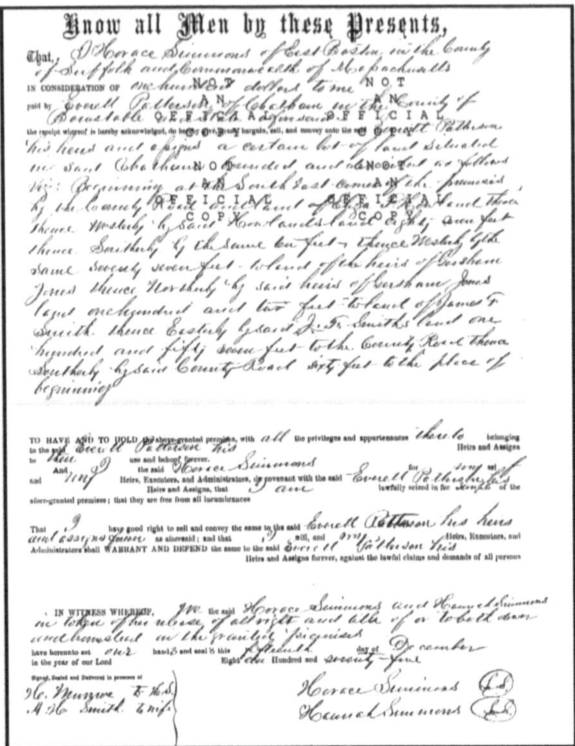

Fig.4 Copy of original 1875 deed. Public record of Barnstable County Registry of Deeds

The deed states:

I, Horace Simmons of East Boston in the County of Suffolk and Commonwealth of Massachusetts, IN CONSIDERATION OF one hundred dollars to me paid by Everett Patterson of Chatham in the County of Barnstable and State aforesaid, the receipt whereof is hereby acknowledged, do hereby give, grant, bargain, sell, and convey unto said Everett Patterson his heirs and assigns a certain lot of land situated in said Chatham bounded and described as follows Viz:

From that point on, it describes the property in terms of the neighboring properties:

Beginning at the SE corner of premises by the county road & land of Eliza F Howland

Thence westerly by Howland's land 87 feet

Thence southerly by the same 10 feet

Thence westerly by the same 77 feet to land of the heirs of Gershom Jones

Thence northerly by said heirs land 102 feet to land of James F Smith

Thence easterly by JF Smith's 157 feet to the county road

Thence southerly by the road 60 feet to the place of the beginning

Following those instructions, a reconstruction of the original 1875 plot plan is shown below in Figure 5, alongside the 1996 plot plan. To situate the property precisely, one has to study old maps where the lots of land were marked with stone markers, existing fences, and the names of the neighbors. As a result, I spent many hours in the bowels of the Atwood House Museum and the Eldredge Library. I studied the census records, noting that the order of entries the census-taker made in his book followed a path down Main Street corresponding to the landowner names on the old maps.

As I conducted all these studies, I wondered who this ghost might have been.

In the story, Cliff Stone intuited that the ghost's name was Missy. I must confess, that was my doing. I hung an empty picture

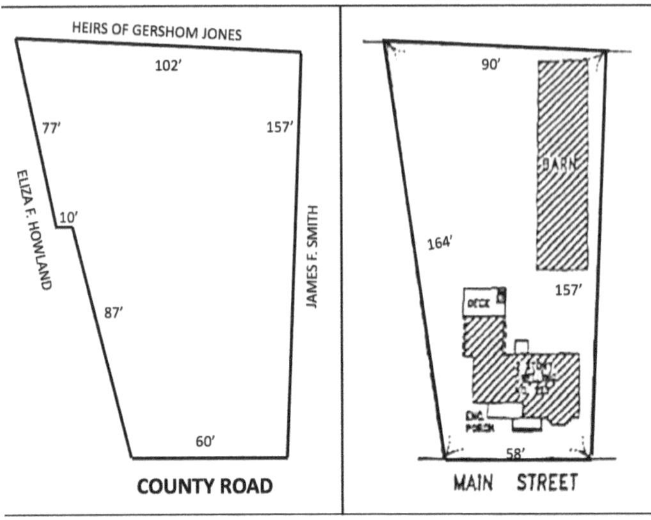

*Fig.5 1875 (left) and 1996 (right) plot plans. Current plan
from DesLauriers & Associates, Walpole, MA*

frame from the garage in the family room and labeled it as the
ghost "Missy." It wasn't until later that summer that I discovered
one of the original owners of the house was a woman who grew up
in the neighborhood and lived in the house most of her life—her
name was Mercie!

Strange things were indeed happening. Dicky Doo and
the Don'ts described it best in their 1958 song— nee nee na na
na na nu nu.

10

Those Who Walked the Back Stairs

The house was built soon after Captain Everett and Mrs.
Mercie Hammond Patterson purchased the land. We can't know
exactly when because, in those days, the county only kept records
of land—there were no building permits nor building inspectors

with books full of codes to be followed. The Victorian architecture is decidedly European—Italianate with a touch of Second Empire French.

No record exists of who the builder might have been, but in that era, Victorian pattern books were widely published in the United States, and sawmills were processing the timber resources of the vast forests. In fact, with European forests largely harvested, a lucrative export business developed in the colonies. Ships arrived with iron tools or red brick from European factories and returned with their holds filled with salted fish and lumber.

The records that trace the ownership of the land from Everett and Mercie Patterson in 1875 back to William Nickerson in 1672 have been lost to posterity. The early deeds, like the Nickerson purchase from the Indians, were kept in the Plymouth County Registry of Deeds. Once Barnstable County was founded in 1685, the subsequent records for Chatham (Monomoit) were kept there.

Unfortunately, a disastrous fire in 1827 destroyed most of Barnstable County's accumulated volumes from 1685 to 1827. Thus, we can trace the Nickerson family's sale of any of the land for 24 years (from 1661 to 1685) in Plymouth County and the purchase of that land for 48 years (from 1827 to 1875) in Barnstable County, but 142 years of land sale deeds (from 1685 to 1827) were lost in the fire.

What we do know is that the daughter to whom William Nickerson first deeded some of his property was married to Robert Eldred. That's significant because the Eldredge name also looms large in Chatham history, and the property on which the house was eventually built some 200 years later was in the name of the widow Priscilla Eldredge. (The Eldredge name is spelled both with and without the ending "ge" on different deeds.)

Priscilla Eldredge sold the land to Sylvester Small. His daughter, Reliance, inherited the land and sold it to Horace Simmons. Simmons sold it to Everett Patterson for the kingly sum of 100 dollars.

The year was 1875. The land was still vacant. The country had grown from 13 British colonies to the independent, federated republic of the United States. Ten years had passed since the end of the Civil War and Lincoln's assassination, and Americans were looking forward to a new era of prosperity.

Everett and Mercie had been married for 14 years when they bought the land in 1875. They had lost their six-year-old son, Everett, six years before and had their second son, Lester, two years before the purchase.

Everett was a sea captain with a scallop schooner whose family came from Nantucket. Mercie, the daughter of John and Mercy Hammond of Chatham, had grown up not far from the new Mansard Victorian home she and Everett built on the property they had just acquired.

In the fictional story, Mercie Badishall remained in the house until her death, waiting for her husband to return from sea. In reality, Mercie Patterson lived all but the last 9 years of her 94-year life in the Old Village of Chatham, 48 of those years in *The House*.

In his drug-induced state, Cliff Stone imagined her playing in the backyard when the last remaining wigwam was still there—not so far-fetched.

In the fictional story, Everett Badishall was lost at sea. In reality, Everett Patterson died of natural causes in 1923. That was when Mercie went to live in Attleboro, Massachusetts, with her son Lester, who no doubt cared for her those last 9 years of her life.

Everett and Mercie Patterson are buried at the seaside cemetery in Chatham.

We can trace the ownership of all those who walked the back stairs of that house after Everett and Mercie. The next owner, Flossie Brown, lived in the house for 25 years. Her husband Harold used the garage out back where he ran a bicycle shop and made whirly gigs. His name is permanently engraved in the cement floor of the garage. He was also a school bus driver for the town and ran Brown's Transportation Parties. Photos of him and Flossie and his enterprises are shown in Figure 6 below. Note that his phone number had only three digits.

Flossie sold the property to Kathryn Morrison (Quigley), who lived there for only four years before moving up by Ryders Cove with her third husband. She was a wealthy woman in the insurance business and lived into her nineties.

Kathryn sold the property to E. Patrick and M. Evelyn Sullivan. They ran the house as the *Seabreeze Bed and Breakfast for a few years.* The old-fashioned night latch locks are still bolted to the

Fig.6 Harold and Flossie Brown and Harold's enterprises. Photos Courtesy of Isabel LaPorte.

inside of the bedroom doors. The Sullivans raised three children in the 15 years that they lived there. Patrick built and refurbished homes on Crowell Street and Holway Street.

The Sullivans' middle child, Mark, lives on the Cape and regularly visits his deep Chatham roots. He once lived at one of Kathryn Morrison's properties at Ryder's Cove and in a boat house on Mill Pond. At one point, he lived in the Sanders cottage on Morris Island Road that belonged to one of the founders of the Lockheed-Sanders electronics conglomerate.

Mark Sullivan has been granted permanent parking privileges in the backyard of *The House* where he once rode his red Western Flyer wagon.

The Sullivans sold the house to Linda and Jim Simonitsch. She was a well-known Chatham art teacher and artist, and every spring, she decorated flower boxes on the window sills facing Main Street with the most magnificent splash of annual flowers.

She also served as a docent for the murals at the Chatham Historical Society's Atwood House Museum. She and her husband kept chickens at one end of the garage, and he planted a prize-winning field of dahlias in the backyard. His name is also carved permanently in the cement floor of the cellar. They both taught in the Chatham School System and raised their family in the house.

Twenty-nine years after they bought the house from the Sullivans, I purchased it.

11

The Scary Back Stairs

The back stairs that led up from the downstairs kitchen to the haunted second-floor bedroom were more like a ladder than a set of stairs. The stair treads were barely wide enough to accommodate a full-sized adult foot. They were even scarier on the way down, requiring a Charlie Chaplin-like duck walk to keep from going over the edge. Since they were grossly out of current safety codes, no modification could be made to them without ripping them out and building an entirely new set of stairs, and there simply was not enough room for such a structure. Thus, they exist to this day. Beware.

Fig.7 The scary back stairs

12

The Hidden Ladder to the Attic Hatch

Another odd artifact that was preserved has the look of a crude set of wooden shelves, only three inches deep, built into the wall outside the haunted, back-stairs bedroom. Even though only knick-knacks are stored on them, each shelf is thick enough to support the weight of a fully grown man—and that's exactly what it was designed to do. The bottom of the shelf pulls out from the wall, and the top slides down in a slot to make a perfect step ladder.

In the ceiling above the hidden ladder is a small wooden hatch that can be slid open to reveal the creepy eaves of the attic. The attic is topped by the cap of the Mansard roof.

It's not a stand-up attic. It's a bend-over-here and a crawl-around-there attic. Some illumination came from slivers of light that snuck in through cracks between the eaves of the roof that "sat like the cover of a pressure cooker" and the Mansard sides that hugged the upstairs bedrooms. A single light bulb hung within reach of the hatch. When you pulled the chain that turned it on, the shadows of giant beams that support the roof swung back and forth across the open floor joists. Between the joists was a cotton-like material that served as meager insulation in the 1900's.

If someone were writing a proper ghost story, they'd have the bevy of ghouls meet in that attic.

I inspected every cranny of the attic, looking for artifacts from when Mercie and Everett Patterson lived there, but except for a tin box of old buttons, it had been picked clean by those who came after them and before me.

Still, that ladder, hidden in plain sight as a set of shelves, intrigued me. I made sure to show it off to any visitors, and then I encouraged them to peek into the attic to get the full sense of the house.

On one occasion, I looked up there and saw what looked like a long, dark overcoat stuffed in the corner of the eaves. As I got near it to investigate, I heard a buzzing sound. It took less than 10 seconds from the time I discovered it was a bee hive the size of Texas to when I had scurried back to the hatch, closed it, and jumped down the ladder.

Stowing the ladder back into the wall was my way of denying the newfound dark presence in the attic. I never called Ghostbusters, but I hired a beekeeper from Harwich to deal with the problem. He tried to convince me that bee venom was good for arthritis. I prefer a hot tub.

He was authorized to use any technique he chose to rid the attic of the bees—from queen bee relocation to total annihilation. I moved out during the operation and only asked one question when I moved back in. "Are they gone?"

Fig.8 The Hidden Ladder

13

The Author's Room Bed

One of the interesting artifacts of the house that had a rich history was the bed to which the character Cliff Stone was chained. It originally belonged to a notable neighbor, Josephine Atkins.

Josephine was born July 4, 1887, and lost her mother at the age of two. Since her father, Joseph Atkins, was away on voyages and other overseas business, she was raised in the household of James and Almena Kent. They raised Josephine as their only child in their Main Street home, just three houses away from *The House.*

When she was only 9 years old, her "Uncle James" died while fighting a fire in his barn. Just three years later, her father committed suicide due to the failure of his business ventures. Soon afterward, "Aunt Mena" officially became Josephine's guardian and later legally adopted her.

After high school, Josephine was sent away to "finishing school" in Boston, but she didn't like it and ended up back home, taking care of Aunt Mena in her old age.

After Mena died in 1924, Josephine began studying at Boston University, where she was awarded a Bachelor's degree in Religious Education.

Josephine lived alone on Main Street in the home she inherited from Aunt Mena. She taught Sunday School at Chatham's Methodist Church and became an ordained minister in 1949 at the age of 67.

Josephine lived in the same house almost her entire life, a house filled with treasures brought back from distant places by both her birth father and her "adopted" father. Many of these pieces of china and furniture, paintings, and so forth were donated to the Chatham Historical Society. The Kent-Atkins Room of the Society's old Atwood House Museum was named in her honor.

One exotic piece of furniture that ended up at *The House* rather than the Museum was the so-called Author's Room bed. The testimony of the then-owner, Linda Simonitsch is as follows:

"It was given in payment of a favor done for Josephine Atkins (an ordained minister) whose Father had captained ships to the China Seas. It had been pushed back among furniture, never to be used in her home, on the corner of Main Street where Main Street turns to the right and Shore Road ("The Boulevard") goes left. It had waited for a few years before it could be moved into the upstairs bedroom. The headboard was so high (almost 5 feet), despite a portion of it being sawed off, that it could not be taken up the steep back stairs or maneuvered around the turn in the front stairway. When a window was taken out, it was taken in!

"This double bed would have been 'cottage furniture' from the Victorian Era elaborately painted to represent different woodgrains, and in this case, accented with lines of hunter green for interest. The painting was done in such a way as to give a trompe d'oeil effect of raised panels and designs—although some beds of that period had intricate raised panels and designs. The footboard was a smaller partner to the headboard, and the legs were massive (almost mission-style like) with spindle adornments on the caps. We added a pseudo-Victorian light fixture to obscure where part of the headboard was missing. For this type of furniture, there was no success like excess!"

The Author's Room bed is shown in Figure 9.

Fig.9 The Author's Room bed with the "ghostly" dress form found in the closet

14

Restoration

In 1998, a Campton, New Hampshire artist named Philip Lonergan (of Lonergan Woodworking) took on the job of restoring the house to its former beauty and grandeur. His objective was to create the look of a traditional 19th-century Mansard Victorian with Italianate and Second Empire features.

He succeeded spectacularly.

The aluminum siding was replaced with traditional clapboard. He recreated the intricate brackets, cornices, and trim,

Fig.10 Lonergan Woodworking contemplating the 1998 renovation

handmaking the corbel brackets with their tear-drop accents. His only error was pointed out harshly by an elderly woman residing in the Old Village passing by who said. "You cannot paint the front door bright purple!"

Thirteen years passed before the interior of the house was refurbished by Gable Building of Chatham. A Concord, Massachusetts architect named Michael Rosenfeld was called in to create a modern interior design while maintaining its 19th–century charm. The interior footprint remained the same. The plan was to preserve the horsehair plaster walls and the dining room's high tin ceiling, but both crumbled under the slightest rehab provocation.

What was found inside the crumbling interior walls brought more speculation of life in the old days of the residents. Newspapers from the early 1900s advertised everything from $28 Wurlitzer

Washing Machines to $5 Miracle Cures. We found antique bottles that no doubt carried some of those cures. Two perfectly preserved buggy whips must have been abandoned when motorized transportation replaced the horse and carriage.

A surprising discovery was that the interior walls of the front parlor had been invaded by the knurly branches of the ivy growing outside the front of the house.

One mysterious find was a silver spoon from the Brigham's Hotel and Restaurant in Boston. The Brigham was built on the site where the Sons of Liberty planted the so-called Liberty Tree as a sign of their opposition to King George. It was designated sacred ground. A hundred years after the American Revolution, the Brigham was one of Boston's most popular and exclusive hotel restaurants. A resident of *The House* must have made a trek up to Boston and taken home a souvenir to commemorate the trip. We found your spoon, ghost.

I must admit that once the house was restored, the ghosts ceased to make their presence known. In the renovation, several of the odd-shaped cubbies and rooms were framed into functional spaces. One such space was the dark upstairs closet, where Cliff Stone first encountered the dress form of the ghost Mercie. It was converted into a bright, white half-bath. That was likely the time when Mercie's spirit finally abandoned *The House*.

15

The Surfmen

At nighttime, if you look out the back windows of the house, you see the sweep of the lighthouse beacon across the top of the trees. It serves as a constant reminder of Chatham's maritime history. In the novel, Missy refers to a surfman who told her that her husband was not returning from sea.

In the actual history of the house, Mercie Patterson's husband, Captain Everett Patterson, was a scallop fisherman who came from a Nantucket maritime family but was never lost at sea.

Still, surfmen were an important part of life in Chatham in the late 1800s. They were members of the U.S. Life-saving Service, which grew out of the Massachusetts Humane Society and preceded the U.S. Coast Guard by 37 years.

Typically, surfmen were fishermen or sailors who were familiar with launching boats in the surf. They would patrol the beaches—especially in storms—looking for ships in distress. If the ships ventured too close to land, they would light flares to warn them. If a ship were in trouble, a rescue team would deploy—sometimes as night approached—to lend assistance or to perform a "cold water" rescue. The surfmen were also skilled at resuscitation, and some were so kind as to bring foreign sailors into their homes for a warm meal and bed for the night.

Thousands of mariners were saved by the extraordinary efforts of the surfmen. Yet, not all surfmen survived, and not all shipwrecked mariners were saved. A quote from Agnes Edwards' 1918 book says it best:

Far out to sea on every hand there is a moaning which neither wind can stifle nor sunshine allay—the moaning of a perpetual dirge for those who have perished along this crystal coast.

The unofficial motto of the U.S. Lifesaving Service was

"You have to go out, but you don't have to come back."

The true story of *The House on Main Street* is rich with history. Whether it is haunted or not is in the mind of the beholder and the heart of the believer. The spirits who might swirl around the Old Village could be the Monomoits who occupied the land for centuries, or they may be descendants of the English and French explorers that first came in the 1600s.

Among those who lived in *The House*, Everett Patterson, who lived there for 48 years of his married life, would be a likely ghost to haunt it, but more so would be his wife Mercie Hammond Patterson, who grew up in the Old Village—on the lands the Monomoits occupied, the explorers visited, the Pilgrims settled, and where she spent the bulk of her life.

At the writing of this Afterword in 2024, I have enjoyed the company of the ghosts that haunt the property for an additional 29 years. I have also enjoyed sunrises at the cliff overlooking Lighthouse Beach, the Fourth of July Parade, Friday-night band concerts in Gould Park, the art galleries, the magnificent Eldredge Library, the daily catch of fresh fish and lobster, the ever-present sweep of the lighthouse beacon, the starry skies, the ocean—rolling and roaring—the shifting shoals, the friends I've made, the tourists who stopped by to sample lemonade from the stand made by kids in my family, and the love that my family brought there.

I celebrate all of it and commemorate my 29th year in *The House on Main Street* by writing this book. – Joseph K. DeRosa

FINIS

BIBLIOGRAPHY

Ancestry. *Search.* Retrieved July 4, 2024 from ancestry.com/search/?searchOrigin=navigation_header.

> An Ancestry.com search of Mattaquason revealed he was known as "Old Sagamore" and his son's Indian name was Towsowet. It's interesting to note how the weight of English culture influenced the name of Towsowet, son of Mattaquason, to become John Quason on the deed. John was 42 years old when the land deal was finalized.

Banner, Stuart. *How the Indians Lost Their Land, Law, and Power on the Frontier.* Cambridge: First Harvard University Press, 2007.

> This book draws the distinction between the presumption that the transfer of land from American Indians took place through violent conquest when, in many cases, it was through consensual agreements. This was especially true in the case of Chatham lands.

Barnstable County Registry of Deeds. "Search Registry Records." Retrieved July 4, 2024, from search.barnstabledeeds.org/ALIS/WW400R.HTM?WSIQTP=SY00

> Land deeds and land court records from 1742 for Chatham are available here. Unfortunately, many of the records before 1827 were destroyed in a fire. Chatham records before 1681 were stored in Plymouth County

Briney, A. *A Brief History of the Age of Exploration.* ThoughtCo. Retrieved July 4, 2024, from thoughtco.com/age-of-exploration-1435006#toc-the-birth-of-the-age-of-exploration

Chatham Smartphone Tour. "Champlain Monument." eTour #43. Retrieved July 4, 2024 from etourchatham.org/champlain.html.

> Discusses a Stage Harbor Road plaque commemorating de Champlain.

Champlain, Samuel de. *The Voyages of Samuel De Champlain — Volume 02*. Translated by Charles P. Otis. Project Gutenberg eBook #6749, 2004, updated 2015. Retrieved July 4, 2024 from gutenberg.org/ebooks/6749

> Samuel de Champlain was not only an explorer but a prolific writer and cartographer. The translation of his accounts of his journeys to the New World makes for exciting reading.

Craven, Jackie. *Picturesque Italianate Architecture in the U.S.* Thought-Co. Apr. 5, 2023. Retrieved July 4, 2024, from thoughtco.com/the-italianate-house-style-178008.

Craven, Jackie. *Historic Second Empire Architecture in Photos.* ThoughtCo. Aug. 27, 2020. Retrieved July 4, 2024, from thoughtco.com/second-empire-architecture-history-and-photos-178044

CULTURA COLECTIVA. "The untold story of the disease the Pilgrims brought to the New World." Retrieved July 4, 2024 from culturacolectiva.com/en/history/pilgrims-disease-decimation-native-american-population/

Edwards, Agnes. *Cape Cod Old and New.* Boston: Houghton Mifflin, 1918.

> Chapter XIII is devoted to the life and legends associated with the Life Saving Service.

Historic Chatham, "Chatham's Wampanoag History," Chatham 300 Historic Site Plaque. Retrieved July 4, 2024 from historic-chatham.org/plaques300_12.html.

> Plaque at the Nickerson Family Association, Orleans Road in Chatham, states that Wampanoag descendants remain throughout the Cape and Islands, most notably at Aquinnah and Mashpee, and that there are descendants of Wampanoag among the many Nickersons and other old Cape Cod families.

Historic Ipswich. "The Great Dying 1616–1619. Retrieved July 4, 2024, from historicipswich.net/2023/11/17/the-great-dying/

Locklear, Rebecca. *The Surfman's Daughter, Growing Up in a Cape Cod Village 1904–1929*. Coppell, TX: Shaket Books and Art, 2022.

This book gives several vignettes in the life of Ernest Eldredge, "The Skipper," who was a member of the Life-Saving Service.

Margaritoff, Marco. *The Devastating History of Diseases That the Pilgrims Brought to America.* Edited by Adam Farley. All That's Interesting, November 23, 2021. Retrieved July 4, 2024, from allthatsinteresting.com/pilgrim-plagues

Here is a discussion of the plagues that beset the natives as well as the King James decree saying it was God's will.

Monbleau, Marcia J. *A Home on the Rolling Deep, The Stories of Eight Sea Captains.* Chatham: The Chatham Historical Society, 1996.

This small monograph gives the transcription of several sea captains. One of them, Seymour Patterson, was the younger brother of Everett Patterson. His father told him to "go out in the world and get your living, and treat everybody as you wish to be treated, and pay your honest debts." No doubt, he gave his older son, Everett, the same advice.

Morris, Josh. "Before the Pilgrims: Champlain in Chatham," *Atwood Log, Newsletter of the Chatham Historical Society* Spring/Summer (2023): p6

More on the exploits of de Champlain

Pacun, Norm. Big Book. Chatham: Chatham Historical Society, in Eldredge Library, Chatham, MA.

This limited-edition book, housed in the Eldredge Library in Chatham, gives the history of each home *in the Old Village.*

Plymouth County. "Registry of Deeds Search." Retrieved July 4, 2024, from titleview.org/plymouthdeeds/

The early Plymouth Colony deeds (including Chatham) are recorded here up until 1681. After 1686, the deeds were recorded in the Barnstable County Registry of Deeds. 1685 to 1827.

Smith, William C. *The History of Chatham Massachusetts, Formerly the Constabulewick or Village of Monomoit, Third Edition.* Chatham: Chatham Historical Society, 1981.

Almost all of the material in this Afterward came from Smith's History of Chatham. He thoroughly researched the primary sources and put together a comprehensive history of Chatham.

Wood, Timothy J. *Breakthrough, The Story of Chatham's North Beach.* Chatham: Hyora Publications, Inc. Revised edition, May 1, 2002.

This book discusses not only the 1987 breakthrough in Nausett Beach, known locally along the Chatham coast as North Beach, but also the history of the beach that dates back to the times of the Norsemen and European explorers. He even mentions the sale of land across from the break to William Nickerson from the Indians.

Young, Jean. "Mariner Oscar Nickerson Recounts Blizzard at Sea," *Atwood Log, Newsletter of the Chatham Historical Society* Fall/Winter (2017/2018): p6

ACKNOWLEDGEMENTS

Much thanks to a number of talented people for helping me as I wrote this story: my mentor Virginia Aronson who made numerous suggestions during the development of the book and carefully edited the final draft; my first readers, Tara Williams and Mary Levenson, accomplished writers in their own right; the many colleagues who helped me hone my writing skills, especially Gloria Barsamian, John Chamberlain, Frank Dubus, Rebecca Gautreaux, D.J. Kelly, John Poignant, and Ernie Stricsek.

The people at three remarkable institutions taught me that natural ability in writing was only the precursor to telling a compelling story. At Grub Street in Boston, The Fine Arts Work Center in Provincetown, MA, and Eckerd College's Writers in Paradise in St Petersburg, Florida, I studied under exceptional authors such as Salvatore Scibona, Andre Dubus III, Nick Flynn, Michael Koryta, and Luis Alberto Urrea. In a number of intensive workshops, they gave me a dousing and a dunking in storytelling.

I would be remiss not to thank my wife, Anne, for her cogent advice and her unending support of my work—invaluable in bringing this and much of my other work to fruition. She is proof positive that the literary life is not the full measure of living.

ABOUT THE AUTHOR

Joseph K. DeRosa is an award-winning writer of fiction and nonfiction. His work has been published in journals and short story anthologies. Before dedicating full-time to writing, he traveled extensively throughout Europe, Australia, Asia, and the United States as a communications engineer and computer scientist. He and his wife, Anne, currently split their time in the blissful paradises of Cape Cod and South Florida—and Paris always awaits.